SUNSET & VINE

LOOSE LIPS

SUNSET & VINE

LOOSE LIPS

A novel by

Per Hampton

FIRST GLOBAL PRESS LLC EDITION, FEBRUARY 2016

This is a work of fiction. Names, characters, businesses, organizations, places, events, and incidents are either the product of the author's imagination or are used fictitiously. Any resemblance to actual persons, living or dead, is a coincidence

ISBN 13: 978-0-9972725-0-5 (paperback)
ISBN 13: 978-0-9972725-1-2 (hardcover)

Book design by Adam Robinson
Cover design by Emery Hampton and Adexyroy

FIND OUT MORE AT WWW.PERHAMPTON.COM

Printed in the United States of America
10 9 8 7 6 5 4 3 2 1

To Mother, Dad,
and my nephews Jimmy and William

“Dream as if you’ll live forever. Live as if you’ll die today.”
—James Dean

“To be kind is the most powerful act in the universe.”
—Per Hampton

CONTENTS

Chapter One

STORMY WEATHER

"Ad Lucem-Pax Tectum."

"Into the light—Peace be with you."

An ancient Roman phrase usually reserved for the most corrupt of a corrupted society.

Neon lights admired their shimmering reflections in a patchwork of rain-filled puddles, spread out across the dark, wet sidewalks of Hollywood's legendary Sunset Boulevard.

It's 5:15 a.m. on a cold January morning. L.A.'s rainy season was upon it and this year's stormy El Nino was in full hell-raising, diva mode. The fierce thunderstorm slung heavy rain drops at full throttle, sideways, as it pounded deserted streets.

"The diner will be packed this morning. I've got to be super alert, I could really pick up some great tips today," Hollywood waitress, Dotty Henderson, spoke to herself aloud while driving. A woman of many secrets and mysteries, some of which were unknown even to herself. One being that she had been a high-society, black market baby of the 1940's.

Her reference to "tips" was not of the monetary kind. Although greed lurked just below the surface, information was the driving force behind her mental note.

Tinged with a little fear, and a healthy dose of suspicion, the long-time Schwab's waitress cautiously drove her old, gray Volvo as if it were an exposed cat operating in stealth mode, slinking and surveying the dark lonely streets of Central Hollywood wound up and ready to pounce.

The car's noisy windshield wipers swooshed wildly from right to left, their robotic thrashing and thumping sound overshadowed the steady hum of the car's engine, loud enough to compete with the terrifying crackle of heavy thunder. The blades struggled to clear the torrential downpour from the car's windshield.

"I'll dash to the bank on my lunch hour. I have to make that big deposit today." She carries on her solo conversation. Momentarily lost in the bliss of adding a thirty thousand dollar check to her ever-growing secret bank account.

"Excellent! There's a spot right in front. Now, if I can only see through this goddamn blinding rain," Dotty mumbled with a sigh of relief upon arriving at her destination, the iconic Schwab's Diner on Sunset Boulevard and Vine Street. The bright red neon "Schwab's" sign flooded down upon the car in the early morning stormy darkness.

Parking was clearly not her forte, and the heavy rain made it all the more challenging. She commenced her routine of pretending her driving skills would succeed in not adding any additional dents to her already beat up rear fender. She gently forced the car's gear shift into reverse and eased backwards while listening for the familiar "thump" from behind that alerted her that contact had been made between her rear bumper and the car behind.

"Perfect!" Sighing with a smile, as her concentration struggled between the joyous flirting of today's banking duties and the more mundane chore of parking.

Switching the car's ignition off, Dotty leaned over to the passenger side while reaching down to the darkly lit floor in search of her umbrella. Stationing her eyes just above the car's weathered dash board. "Can't be too careful in the streets at this hour." She says suspiciously to herself as she braces one hand on the dashboard's cracked padding for balance.

Her instincts urged her to keep a watchful eye out for strangers on the quiet, darkly lit street.

Suddenly, the bright flash from an oncoming car's high beam lights glared towards her. It was heading directly for her, the brilliant lights temporarily blinding her.

"Oh my God! That car is going to crash into me! Oh my God! No!" she screamed, cowling down in the car seat with both arms pulled tightly together, hands clasped around her face, anticipating the deadly impact. Just as suddenly, the sound of screeching brakes triggered her reflex to look up in the direction of the terrifying sound. Dotty sat upright, her eyesight blurred with the bright spots caused by the glaring headlights. She blinked rapidly in an attempt to clear her vision. Seconds later, she was able to see just long enough to catch a glimpse of a black Mercedes speeding away.

"Jesus, I thought that car was going to kill me!" Panting heavily as her olive complexion paled with the flush of life-threatening fear.

"I've seen that car before." Momentarily taking stock of her trembling hands gripping the car's steering wheel. Dotty spoke aloud what her instincts were silently communicating to her, "That was no accident. That goddamn threat was meant for me." Her salty tongue reflecting her sense of panic.

She jogged her memory into action as it reviewed her previous morning's drive to work. The details had been etched into her mind, recalling the nervousness of peering into her car's rear view mirror and seeing the headlights that had followed her every turn. Now she was convinced it was the same black Mercedes with blacked out windows that had tailed her yesterday morning from Burbank through the isolated Cuhuenga Pass.

This realization sent an additional shock wave of fear through her.

"Someone knows," she admitted to herself.

"I hope no one has found me out! I'll be ruined … and in a helluva lot of trouble."

Dotty had covert reasons to be paranoid regardless of the time of day, or location for that matter.

"That's it! I've made up my mind. I'll tell Ralph I want a gun, and I want it this week." Trying to calm her jittery nerves with the thought of a pistol for protection.

"I'll just tell him it's because I'm driving to work so early in the morning and I'd feel safer having one. No need to mention being followed, he might start asking too many questions and I can't afford that right now."

Truth is she had potential enemies … lots of them. Her only safety net was clinging to an evaporating sense of anonymity.

"I've got to be extra careful from now on."

"Someone in that car knows my secret."

Chapter Two

BITTER FIGHT

Dotty sat in her car, stunned, more from the possibility of having been found out than the calculated death threat. Seeking to compose herself, she briefly entertained regret, "I should have stayed on my old work schedule along with everyone else. Is my secret deal-making becoming too risky?"

Following the angry, jealous confrontation with Vivien, the fiancée of Schwab's manager, Sam O'Brien, Dotty had made the decision to avoid coming to work at her usual hour in an attempt to prevent any possible trouble caused by the two of them being alone together. Despite harboring feelings of uneasiness about the earlier hour, it was for the best.

"I can't allow petty relationships to get in my way right now, there's too much at stake. Besides, my relationship with Sam was only about fun sex." A tawdry admission from such an under-the-radar, middle-aged waitress. One who had grown up being referred to as "not much in the looks department, but she has a great personality." A universal kiss of death for dating.

The relentless thunderstorm and what appeared to be a purposeful threat from that mysterious black car made her feel like a target. The sum of the morning portended events to come.

Dotty tried shrugging off her jitters, but it just wasn't working. Her nerves were on edge. Something just didn't feel right this morning, and her "third eye" was trying to warn her.

"Has someone found me out? Some of the regulars have been a bit distant lately, especially the three girls. I'll pay close attention to their behavior today to see if they are suspicious."

Those were questions she posed to herself while killing time during her solitary half hour alone before the other employees arrived.

Life's dividends had always paid well for those that remained attuned to and respected natural intuition versus robotically adhering to the brain's logic. Repeated attempts to brush her uneasiness off as just another angle of guilt that attempted to gnaw at her failed. There was no denying that the mysterious car had rattled her normally cool, calculating persona.

The Hollywood waitress, wet and nervous, dashed from the car to get out of the heavy rain. Sunset and Vine was eerily silent except for this morning's violent rumble of thunder accompanied by flashes of lightning bolts so bright they turned night into day. The storm terrified her almost as much as being followed.

Quickly closing the front door of the restaurant behind her, she simultaneously switched on the diner's front lights. The neon in the window made a sparking sound as the bright red and green "Schwab's Hollywood" sign came to life. Dotty then dove into her morning routine. People often find refuge in predictable habits when rattled. She was no different.

"Wow, this storm is terrible! I hope it lets up before it'stime to open." Talking aloud to herself for comfort and assurance that all was well, while mentally trying to fight off an increasing crescendo of fear.

She attempted to release some of the tension on her soaked raincoat and umbrella with an overtly aggressive shake to rid them of as much moisture as possible. Tidying herself from the rain, she made her way to the diner's back kitchen; her mind still stubbornly focused on the car that had followed her to work, twice. Pondering if this could very well be the downfall of her very lucrative secret side job.

Glancing around the quiet, empty diner overwhelmed her with a momentary sense of profound loneliness that placed her on the edge of tears. Dotty's thoughts of redemption and remorse were as fleeting as the lightning flashes that filled the stormy sky that morning.

Making her way to the back of the kitchen. "I need a good strong cup of fresh coffee. That'll get my mind off this nonsense." As she began to sing her favorite feel good "happy song":

"Somewhere over the rainbow, way up high
There's a land that I heard of once in a lullaby
Somewhere over the rainbow, skies are blue way up high
And the dreams that you dare to dream really do come true"

Flipping the switch on to the back kitchen lights, she hummed and sang to herself.

Suddenly, a loud bang rang out from the direction of the front door.

Dotty jumped, swirled around towards the noise as her fingers lost their grip on the coffee cup she was holding, sending it crashing to the floor. Certain she heard what sounded like the front door open and shut. At first startled, then exhaling a sigh of relief, she assumed it was the arrival of Jacques, Schwab's Valet.

"Whoa, thank goodness someone else has finally arrived! I'm shaking like a leaf!" Assuming it was her French co-worker.

"I don't think I will ever be comfortable being in this place alone so early in the morning, even if it is for only 30 minutes."

It was still pitch black outside at this hour and her paranoia had gotten the best of her.

"Being here when it's this quiet just plain gives me the creeps." Admitting to herself, then calling out, "Good morning, Jacques, how are you."

Running her hands up and down her arms and shoulders in an attempt to soothe her raised goose bumps and shivering nerves.

Hesitating, then whispering to herself in a muffle, "It must be Jacques."

Once again raising her voice. "Good morning, Jacques!" Giving it a second try. Hoping for a reply in a relieved, upbeat happy tone. There was no answer.

"I'm sure I heard the door open and close."

"Hello, anybody there?"

Dotty's eyes suddenly grew large with an expression of fright when there was no response. Trying to reconcile in her mind what could only have been cold fresh air wafting through the kitchen doorway shortly after hearing the sound of the door open and close.

"I definitely felt a cold breeze blowing blow in from the front," Dotty thought to herself, her mind now working overtime in an attempt to rationalize what her senses had already acknowledged as fact, thus triggering that ancient part of the human brain known as the amygdala and it's primordial "Fight or Flight Response."

Her body responded by pumping itself full of epinephrine. Taking a deep sigh then filling her lungs with unneeded deep gasps of air, thus in turn triggering a sense of panic, her heavy breathing commanded her heartbeat to accelerate faster and faster. The color in her face alternated between pale and crimson, and her voice cracked.

"OK ... guys ... I heard you come in. I know you're in there. Please stop joking, this is not funny. I'm already scared out of my wits just being alone here at this hour of the morning!"

Secretly hoping Jacques or, out of desperation, even Sam was playing a cruel joke on her. There was no answer.

In an attempt to convince herself that there was nothing to worry about, "Could I have just imagined hearing the door open? Am I hearing things? Maybe your hearing's going bad, ol' girl." Speaking to herself with a contrived, forced smile. An effort at soothing ragged nerves. Her subconscious wasn't buying it, not for a second. It was not about to forget the fresh cold breeze that could only have come from the outside.

A few seconds later Dotty heard the sound of someone or something stumble into the side of a dining room table, followed by the sound of rolling glass salt and pepper shakers toppling over and shattering as they fell to the floor. The crashing sound was immediately followed by the diner's front lights going black!

Frozen with fear, she stopped dead in her tracks, looking around for a weapon to protect herself. Her terrified eyes made contact with the cooking knives hanging on the wall on the other side of the kitchen. Unfortunately, they were near the doorway that led to the front of the diner.

"Dammit! Did I forget to lock the door? I'm so damned shaken up by that car following me this morning I can't think straight. Dear Lord, please, please don't let me get robbed." Praying to herself in a hushed tone.

Searching for a safe place to hide, fear began to take hold of her entire being. Her hands became clammy and began to shake like those of a severe alcoholic who's been without a drink for twenty-four hours. She tried not to breath too loudly, frightened that whoever it was might hear her, then know exactly where she was hiding.

"Oh God, what am I going to do? It's a goddamn burglar!"

The only other exit from the kitchen to the outside was dead bolted and the key was in the cash register. If it was a robbery, she was trapped.

"Whoever you are … I've got a gun and I'm not afraid to use it!" Lying through her teeth, something she definitely knew how to do. Running to the wall on the other side of the kitchen away from the doorway as silently as possible, she scrambled to click off the light switch.

"At least if it's dark they won't be able to find me right away."

Just as she hit the off switch, background light from the outside filtered through the diner's large front windows, creating a serene aura in the front dining area. The outside light cast a yellow flickering of shadows as the leaves danced wildly from the wind and rain in front of the street lamps. The echoing shadows shown through the doorway, casting a long, ominous path on the dark kitchen floor.

The strange image fleetingly reminded Dotty of a film noir movie or childhood memories of lying in bed and watching the light and shadows from outside her windows play on the floor while she drifted off to sleep.

Brought back to the danger of the moment by the sound of footsteps emanating from the front, she announced, "I don't have any money here. Please, take whatever you want from the front. I haven't see you! I'll never say a word!"

Thinking quickly, "If he falls for that, I can make it to my coat where my cell phone is in my pocket, then call the police! That fucking dirty bastard!"

Allowing her devious, double crossing nature to momentarily surface.

That's when the voice spoke for the first time, confirming her worst nightmare. One she had tried to keep locked away. "But I'm not after money, you low-life bitch! I've come for a bigger, more valuable prize. You've been a very, very bad girl, and lots of people really, really hate you, Dotty Henderson. I think I might be the one that hates you the most. And I'm here to serve up a big, sweet dish of revenge. bitch! By the way, It's one of my favorite recipes," the tauntingly low voice threatened with a mocking snicker.

Dotty struggled to recognize the voice as she fell shaking backwards then crouched further into the corner between the big stove and a large stainless steel cook's table. The darkest spot she could squeeze into.

"Please, I'm begging you, leave me alone. I haven't done anything to anyone!"

"Oh, but you have. You're rotten to the core and you've destroyed enough lives with your filthy, cheap little side job. No more! You're done with selling peoples" secrets and fucking up their lives! You've sold your last piece of trash, you blood-sucking vermin!" the raspy voiced intruder spit out.

"Who are you? What have I ever done to you? I'm … just a little nobody waitress. I really don't know what you are talking about! I wouldn't hurt anybody. Whoever you are, please, you've mistaken me for someone else. I'm begging you, please don't hurt me, I have a young daughter and a husband!"

"Poor little Dotty, you obviously have me mixed up with someone who gives a shit about your stinking, miserable life! God, it's delicious to hear you beg! So, all of a sudden … your family is important to you. You didn't seem to think so highly of them when you were busy screwing over others and destroying lives while peddling your filthy gossip for profit, did you?"

Now sobbing, Dotty mumbles, "But, I … I don't understand. What are you talking about?" Using her most manipulative tone of self pity.

"Your little secret is over! I'm gonna slit your evil throat from ear to ear like a pig on a barbecue pit, then watch with joy as every drop of blood drains from your evil corpse! You've taken everything from me, and I intend to take what's most precious to you: your ruthless, parasitic life!"

Realizing she had to do something other than beg if she was going to survive this ordeal, Dotty yelled out to remind whoever it was, "I told you, I've got a gun, don't make me use it! Stay away from me! I will shoot! People on the street will hear it and call the police! If you leave now I won't say word to anyone. I promise! I don't know who you are, but you are really messing with the wrong woman! I'll shoot if you come any closer!" Trying to convince herself that she might bluff her way out of this nightmare with a hollow threat.

The menacing stranger spit out through clenched teeth, "Greedy little Dotty, you are dumber than you are homely looking. You're out of your league with me, bitch, only you're too stupid to know it. Hollywood can be a very vengeful town when you fuck us over. Better get that gun ready 'cause I've come for revenge and I'm not leaving until I make sure you've breathed your last stinkin' breath of air in this world."

Dotty struggled to control her whimpering.

"Is it money you want? I can give it to you, lots of it." Switching angles and hoping money was worshiped by the stranger as much as it was by her.

"Just let me go to the bank when it opens. I promise you, I'll never say another word to a tabloid again." Finally admitting out of life-threatening fear what she had suspected all along, that her dirty secret dealings had finally caught up with her.

"I didn't mean to hurt anyone … PLEASE, PLEASE you gotta believe me!"

Catching herself sobbing hysterically, she quickly threw her hands over her mouth in an attempt to conceal herself in her hiding place.

"Dear God!" she muffled as she inhaled the longest breath of fear she had ever known after seeing the outline of a shadow standing in the doorway. It cast a long silhouette across the dark room. That beautiful golden glow from the street lamps lit the nightmarish figure from behind.

Dotty still couldn't make out the low, gravely voice. Her mind raced through her past as she fell backwards, crouching beside the large steel cook's table. What had she done? How could she have been so callous with peoples' lives just for money? Who had tracked her down? The answers to these questions would follow her to her grave and beyond.

"Is this how I am going to die?" she asked herself as the reality of the stranger's intent sank in.

Dotty was trapped with no escape, just like so many of the people whose lives she had ruined for selfish monetary gain in her devious, relentless pursuit of money.

A momentary ray of hope appeared when she remembered, "I'm sure Sam or Jacques will be here any minute now. All I have to do is keep talking, stall a little while longer until they get here."

Once again turning to the Lord for something other than her usual prayer for more money, "I'm begging you, dear Lord, please give me one more chance. Just let them get here in time."

"Aren't you at least going to tell me who you are?" mustering to ask through her sniffling whimpers.

"That's a good girl, you dragon-tongued bitch! Keep begging. I like hearing the sound of fear in your voice," said the stranger.

"Oh, Dotty's scared. It won't do you any good! I want to see the pain and fear in your eyes while you suffer. In the same manner you caused so many of your victims to live through."

Carefully eying the shadowy figure move into the kitchen, Dotty caught a glimpse of the huge, monstrous, shiny knife in the stranger's hands. Backing herself further into the corner, she managed to squeeze in another inch. Just like a rat hiding from a big hungry alley cat in the dark. Dotty's wailing only got worse as she tried to muffle her sounds by holding her hand over her nose and mouth out of fear of being heard. Her trembling was so bad she had to grab hold of the table's cold steel leg to steady herself.

Keeping track of the time, the intruder moved quickly. Dotty had been stalked for the last month by the mysterious stranger and they knew exactly when the rest of the morning staff would be arriving. It wasn't hard really. They had attached a SAT NAV device to her car and knew the exact moment she left her house for work every morning. Then, they discreetly monitored her from across the street as she entered Schwab's … alone. Her stalker knew the earliest that either of the other two employees, Sam or Jacques, would arrive wasn't until around 5:45 a.m., or later, allowing them plenty of time to dispatch their swift gift of murderous revenge.

Dotty wasn't even sure if the intruder was a man or a woman. She couldn't tell from the low whispering voice. The only thing she could make out was the trench coat, knit cap, and that terrifying long butcher knife in their hands.

With her eyes wide open and targeted in the direction of every sound or movement made in the darkness, her body's million-year-old evolutionary human instincts were operating on full alert. She desperately tried to blend into the darkness and remain hidden, vowing to amend her ways if she made it out alive. Her mind was half stuck in the limbo of expecting the lights to come on at any moment, thus instantly giving her location away, and trying to comprehend if this nightmare would be her last.

"I never dreamed this much fear could be real," she thought to herself. But it was real and she was living every second of it.

Closing her eyes and praying for forgiveness, "My sweet merciful God, please give me one more chance. I am begging for your atonement. I promise I will live by your word if you spare me from this." Making promises to the Lord that she knew she was incapable of keeping. Her newly found religiosity had simply arrived too late.

A moment later, the dark room was quiet.

"Maybe they've left?" Hoping that some other-worldly miracle had driven whoever it was away. Confident, that her Lord savior had heard her prayers and kindly bestowed mercy upon her, Dotty opened her closed eyes in relief. It was at that frozen second in time that she saw the reflecting light from the street on the massive, long, shining steel blade in the shadowy dark and its life draining silver tip. At this very same moment the cold blade came thrusting down into her warm soft flesh. Dotty immediately thought about how time had slowed down as it was occurring, as if time had almost come to a halt.

The piercing, first stab seared through her body with the force of a falling piano onto her chest. It felt like the knife had been plunged all the way into her body, up to its handle. There was no more pondering or hope, she was going to die. Her life began to flash before her like pictures on a slide projector. Oddly enough, the first images were of the terrible tabloid headlines she had profited from:

"Starlet's secret past as a PROSTITUTE revealed!"

"Hunky Leading man's hidden HUSBAND identified!"

"Film Star commits suicide over secret revelations!"

Breaking through those images were those of a far more motherly vision:

"My poor baby is going to be without a mother." Finally, realizing the unbearable cost of her deeds upon her beloved, beautiful 20-year-old daughter.

The long, thick, cold, steel blade sliced into her body like a hot knife into butter. She tried to scream but no sound came out. Lying in a state of shock from the searing pain, she couldn't even throw her arms up to block the vicious attack or fight her attacker. Her body went limp and numb after the third strike. The strength behind the attack was of such rage she begins to pray for death to come quickly. The violent blade struck her body blow after blow … until, finally, her world started to fade into what seemed like peaceful blackness. In a bizarre twist, Dotty began to relish the feeling of the warm blood flowing over her body, as if it were cleansing away her horrible deeds.

The last words she was to hear in life were from her tormentor in a low, gratifying sense of delight.

"Goodbye, Dotty Henderson, and remember the distance from good to evil is but a thought. Say hello to Hell for me, you evil WHORE!"

Dotty Henderson's reservation at Forest Lawn had been filled.

They found her that morning in a pool of blood, stabbed 23 times, her face covered by the bloodied, screaming headlines of a tabloid stuck to her forehead.

The resulting investigation would release a torrent of secrets and controversy that plunged Hollywood into a state of emergency. It also presented it at it's finest. Nothing is as it appears in this town, and its reality is by far more intriguing and cinematic than its films.

Chapter Three

DREAMING

Police sirens, accompanied by strobing red lights, challenged the dominating storm as they roared through the streets of Hollywood from multiple directions. All headed for Sunset and Vine.

Schwab's manager, Sam O'Brien, had been the first to discover the grisly murder scene. He had become unnerved after arriving for work and finding the front door open with the diner's interior lights off and recognizing Dotty's car parked in front of the entrance. After calling out to Dotty and getting no response, he phoned the police, as well as Schwab's owners.

Hollywood Division homicide detective Rocco Goldman was the first to respond when the call went out as he was already en route to Schwab's for his routine breakfast. A predictable practice after his graveyard shift. The detective found Dotty's butchered body with the knife still plunged into her chest and that sick, bloody, tabloid front page pasted on her forehead.

"Six years I've been working homicide and I've never seen anything like this. Very disturbing, very disturbing!"

He was speaking to his ex-partner Elsa Wagoner. Elsa had immediately been hired by Schwab's owners to find the killer, and had also offered a $25,000 reward.

"Here's the list of morning regulars you asked for." Sam handed the piece of paper to detective Goldman. "Most of them should be here shortly, if they haven't been scared off already by the press."

Rocco reviewed the list of patrons, recognizing that he was familiar with most of them. He had been a part of the early morning breakfast regulars for a little under five years. Silently recalling that he had been served for years by the same sweet woman who now lay, gruesomely murdered, beneath a blood soaked cloth at his feet.

As he scanned the murder scene he began a review of Dotty's life while developing his strategy for the investigation.

Detective Goldman was pleased to have his former partner Elsa unofficially working with him as a private detective. She had retired from the force after her new wife protested about the dangers of being a police officer. Going into business for herself and a private investigator, she had developed a reputation as one of the most competent PIs in the city.

Schwab's owners hired Elsa because they couldn't allow this dark cloud to linger for very long over the establishment. It was bad for business. They needed this murder solved, fast.

It would later be discovered that Dotty died because she had made a living destroying the lives of others. Perhaps someone from that group of unfortunates, many of whom frequented the homey Schwab's, had dealt her what she had secretly, and so ruthlessly, had been dishing out to others. Her weapon of choice was a conniving, vicious tongue. What was worse, this sweet lovable waitress had profited handsomely by it.

Dotty had left behind a beautiful, innocent young daughter, a loving husband, and two million dollars in cash hidden in secret bank accounts. All on the wages of a waitress.

The world would soon learn things aren't always as they seem, especially in this town. A trail of broken hearts and shattered Hollywood lives led straight to sweet little Dotty.

The size of her savings was astounding to all who knew her. As shocking as this revelation was, the rest of her unknown legacy would stun the world. A legacy that even she was unaware of.

Why had what appeared to be, a loving, committed mother, daughter, and wife, at least until Sam had come along, lead such a double life?

She hadn't intended to destroy anyone's lives by being a source of cruel gossip to the tabloids … it just happened and took on a life of its own. She soon learned that the seedier the gossip, the more they paid. It became her mission. Her mistake was to leave all decency behind and pursue an unyielding greed.

She could not blame her imagined slight on a working-class background. She tried though, along with her low self-esteem. She often asked herself, "What was driving me to act this way? A force of instinct maybe? Everyone has them; they shape parts of our personalities."

Dotty, it seems, was compelled to compensate for her imagined inadequacies: her feelings of being a common looking waitress swimming in an ocean of wealth and glamour.

Rocco asked Elsa, "Who would want to kill sweet little Dotty in such a violent manner? I mean, everyone loved Dotty. What was the significance of the tabloid plastered to her forehead?"

As the details of Dotty's secret life unfolded, detective Goldman realized that what would turn out to be the all time mother lode for the Hollywood Police Division had fallen into his hands.

No one could have ever expected this murder to entangle so many high-profile members of the rich and famous. All caught in a murder web connected to a seemingly simple, unassuming waitress. It would rock Hollywood, and indeed all of America's high society, to its foundation, causing many to take a long deep look into the locked closets of lovers and family members. Many found things they wish they hadn't. Others attempted to ignore the secrets they found and go on with their lives.

To say that some of the famous residents of Hollywood would develop a bad case of nerves would be an understatement. The problem so many of the famous were confronted with was that their names had a way of being leaked to the voracious tabloid press. It didn't matter if they were innocent or not. The mere association of their names with the dramatic and grizzly murder meant money for the gossip rags.

Headlines screamed on a daily basis the names of Schwab's regulars.

A business practice that poor departed Dotty knew all too well.

The dirt that was to be exposed from this murder, of a nobody waitress at a legendary Hollywood eatery, would be called a "triple hit"—that of "salacious sex, dirty money for gossip, and revenge murder" by the tabloids.

The investigation retraced Dotty's life as closely as possible. She had waited too late to heed the warning signs that had began popping up. Like being followed not once but twice. Or the subtle change in attitudes by some of the regulars. Too bad for her, she had ignored it.

Looking back, one can see where it all began to unravel.

As fate would have it, Dotty could never have imagined the truly incredible events that lay ahead of her over the next few months. Events that would have changed her life beyond her wildest dreams.

If only she hadn't embraced the dark side with her devious greed. It would take some understanding of who she was and what went on in her private life, every part of it, to comprehend why someone would commit such a heinous crime.

One thing was certain, Dotty Henderson was a driven woman with many, many secrets.

Rocco asked Elsa, "Are you ready for this?"

"I was born ready."

"There are an awful lot of rich, very powerful, famous people that come in here."

"And they will all have to be investigated."

"It's already a feeding frenzy outside."

Turning to a police officer standing inside the diner, "Get those goddamn windows covered right now!" Orders Detective Goldman.

"I want a concealing canvass tunnel put up to take her body out to the coroner's van. And for Christ's sake, tell forensics to take that goddamn knife out of her chest right now!"

"Yes sir, right away, Sergeant Goldman."

"Elsa, scan the prelims. You and I will regroup after all of this noise and flash has gone. I've got to get to her family before the rabid vultures from the press. After all, I knew this woman, saw her almost every morning, knew her daughter and husband. It is the least I can do."

Elsa was a tough ex-cop but even her eyes struggled not to match Rocco's watery eyes. They had lost a dear friend who had been a calming force in a city of chaos.

"Keep those vipers as far away as possible!" Rocco declared before leaving.

The investigation of Dotty Henderson's murder would make her one of the most famous women in Hollywood history. Posthumously of course.

Chapter Four

THE ROAD TO GREED

Dotty's last day of life had begun like any other beautiful, sunny Southern California day.

She had entered a new chapter in life where she felt in control.

"For the first time in my life, I feel smart, sexy, and excited about my future and my beautiful daughter's."

"She will have everything that I didn't. How did I get so lucky to give birth to such a beauty who also happens to be brilliant!"

"I always knew I was destined for a life at the top. It's in my genes."

"I was born to live well, and I am going to make it happen!"

If only she knew the truth behind those frivolous words.

Dotty and Ralph Henderson lived in quaint Burbank.

Burbank was stable, quiet, and convenient to everything Dotty needed … for the moment. As glamorous as it would have been living over the hill in West Hollywood or the Hollywood Hills, she was just too sensitive to the noise and the VERY expensive house prices, far too expensive for her and Ralph. Although just as expensive, "Sherman Oaks was different," her contrived reasoning quantified her obsessive justification with moving to there.

Dotty possessed acute hearing sensitivity that never allowed her to use alarms, and, instead, she relied upon her neighbor's alarm regularly setting off at 4:00 a.m. every morning.

She'd learned to live with her hyper-sensitive hearing. A curse when trying to sleep, this later to be turned into a profitable asset.

The streets of Burbank were rarely full of traffic, even during rush hour. It was a small town surrounded by the megalopolis that was Los Angeles.

Ralph didn't have to rise until 6:00 a.m., but he enjoyed having a daily cup of coffee with his wife of 23 years before she was off for the day.

A seemingly devoted couple, they met when Ralph had stumbled into Schwab's by accident after becoming confused about the name of a restaurant for a business lunch. That's the day he met Dotty and her warm smile. She'd noticed a sparkle in Ralph's eyes after the second cup of coffee. Soon after, he become a regular for lunch. His air conditioner repair job took him all over the west side of the city, thus giving him an opportunity and an excuse to see Dotty during his lunch hour.

That was a long time ago, long before Dotty met Sam O'Brien. If only Sam had taken his management position at Schwab's before she'd met and married Ralph. O'Brien was the kind of guy Dotty thought would never be interested in her. She was wrong, but it was too late in the game for a rewind.

Dotty had to stay focused on the deals she was cooking up to make her rich. A lot was at risk, a lot was to be had, and she was ready for her big payoff in life. Love was the last thing on her mind right now. The greed in her never took a holiday.

"I know I should be thankful. That I should be happy … I don't know why I'm not satisfied," she would often say to herself out loud when alone. It was as if she had this uncontrollable urge that made her rebel against her common sense of being a good person.

She had a devoted, loving husband, a wonderful daughter, and a nest egg that would allow her to finally live the life she felt she deserved, regardless of how she'd gotten it. A life she'd dreamed of as a young girl ages ago when reminiscing about strolling down those beautiful, sleepy, serene streets of Sherman Oaks.

"Dreaming about the beautiful life and those beautiful people inside those beautiful homes."

The reality of all this "beauty" existed only in her head, tucked away in the scientifically proven area of the cerebral cortex identified as fantasy land.

It was a far cry from gritty next door Van Nuys, where she had grown up. Now, years later, she sometimes took the long way home, a drive through Sherman Oaks just for a "look-see" at what was on the real estate market.

Dotty did so because she knew she now had enough cold hard cash to buy almost any house she wanted in Sherman Oaks, any time she wanted, and that would be real soon, "By God!" She smiled as she thought "my day has dawned!" Sherman Oaks was so serene one could almost forget horrible, messy things like murder could touch one of the residents of this faux "Mayberry."

"My life had been hard growing up in Van Nuys in the 1950's, at least hard by the Golden State's standards. It was especially envious for working class kids like me, living next door to "leave it to Beaver," Upper Middle–Class Sherman Oaks," she thought while reminiscing about her childhood.

"Sherman Oaks, and those oh so quiet, meandering streets, lined with big, overbearing oak trees and white picket fences." Letting her obsession with living in Sherman Oaks run wild … a goal set to prove to herself and the world that she was good enough to enjoy what she perceived as the ultimate American dream.

Dotty just wanted to know what it was like to live like those people in her imagination. She wanted to be "one of them."

She never really thought of herself as greedy, and knew she was far from beautiful, yet it was material trappings that motivated her secret endeavors. At least it started out that way.

"It's not just the money now, I've found out that I also love the game. I have to admit, I'm damn good at it. And nobody has a clue. They think I'm just a dumb waitress, but I'll be the one who has the last laugh!" Ending with a chuckle.

Occasionally, when Dotty headed South of Ventura Boulevard onto Laurel Canyon she would think to herself, "How the envy and resentment towards the lifestyle of living in Sherman Oaks is still in me from childhood."

That envy entrenched tough determination.

"To try my hardest with what life had dealt me. I wanted to improve my lot in life, not just accept it." She had no intention of accepting a station in life she felt had been awarded by a mistake of fate.

"I had a high school education, homely looks, even made up, so I was under no false illusions. I was a practical young girl, with good manners, clean hair and nails, and lots of humility. Humility can be a powerful weapon if used properly," she was fond of saying, feeling a sense of pride in her no nonsense approach to life.

Things had played out "OK" she thought, "not great, but … OK, if you're interested in being average. I'm not."

An hour earlier, she had been hosting her favorite dream, only this morning it carried an omen with it.

"God I love driving up my long driveway. Beyond the ivy covered fence towards my beautiful colonial. Mine, all mine, every brick, plank, and blade of grass, 2522 Shady Oaks Circle,

Sherman Oaks, California. Finally, somehow the birds sound more beautiful here, the air fresher, the sky bluer." Smiling at herself while dreaming.

"What's happening? Why is it getting dark outside, it's only morning? I don't understand. I don't like this, something is wrong. I can feel it." Her dreaming smile morphing into a worried grimace.

"Got to wake up. Get up for work … must wake up!' Dotty tossed and turned. Her face displayed a frightened crease in the middle of her forehead. A reflection of the dark clouds of fear gathering in her dream.

Upon awakening she looked down to see her heart furiously pumping as her chest heaved up and down.

"That was a disturbing dream." One of many she had been having as of late.

"Time to get the wheels rolling!" Quipping to Ralph as she bounced out of bed towards the bathroom and shower. Her thoughts racing to map out her mission for the day.

"My stash will be well over the $2 million mark." Money, of course, was first on her list. Continuing her solo conversation:

"Set up a meeting with Jacques. Start low with his offer and let him negotiate up to a point." One or two words escapes her lips loud enough for Ralph to hear.

"Whatcha say honey?" Ralph yelled in her direction.

Ralph sat on the edge of the bed in his polka-a-dot boxers scratching his disheveled hair. In his early forties he was still fit enough to look down and see his belt buckle when standing. Ralph glanced over his shoulder towards the bathroom.

"Oh nothing, just figuring out what I have to do at work today." Dotty raised her voice over the sound of the shower starting.

"I'll fix us some coffee really quick," Ralph mumbled.

"Lover, you are a sweet dear. What would I do with you in the morning!" replied Dotty in the form of a song.

"I like doing this for you in the morning, you work so hard during the day, on your feet all day with all those demanding customers. I know how those rich folks can be. This lets me give you a little well deserved service once a day," he proudly proclaims.

"I'm gonna marry you one day! Oops, I already did! See, you are so wonderful you still make me feel like an excited girlfriend!" She tries to sound flirty.

Dotty was not lying about her feelings towards Ralph. He was a good man and she loved him, but she wanted more. Learning long ago to hide and live with the guilt that reared its monstrous head every so often. Knowing in her heart that Ralph deserved better.

She always felt this way as she scanned her drawer in the daily ritual of selecting which sexy pair of lingerie to be worn. Lingerie not meant for the eyes of her husband.

"Oh, I don't mind most of the customers, honey, they really are nice people for the most part, and they treat me well. Lord knows I wouldn't have stayed this long had it been too bad. I do appreciate your sweetness. You are such a dear to me." Spoken sincerely from a woman with so many secrets, she'd perfected the delicate straddle between honesty, lying, and betrayal like an acrobat on a high wire.

"Goodbye dear, I want to make it through Laurel Canyon before the traffic starts."

Telling Ralph on her way out the door. In truth, she was excited to get to work every morning for many reasons, none of which had anything to do with beating traffic. Dotty's secret agenda began at Schwab's, but certainly didn't end there!

"Have a good day, honey. I'll be home a little late this evening. I have to go out to Malibu," Ralph yells back.

"Mmmm Kiss!"

Throwing her hand towards him with an air kiss over her shoulder without looking back.

Chapter Five

SCHWAB'S

Dotty's carefully selected lingerie had been worn for one set of eyes only, and they were not those of her husband's. They were for Sam O'Brien's, manager of Schwab's Diner.

Owner Mike Brockman politely, but firmly, informed Sam O'Brien when offering him the job of running the restaurant, "Schwab's isn't just any diner, damn it, it's Schwab's! Legendary Schwab's to be exact, and don't you ever forget it! We discover Movie Stars here! How do you like that! How many of them little hole in the walls in your past has reached cultural icon status? In Hollywood no less!"

About a total of none, Sam added up, and decided to fly out from New York City and take a look.

Sam was a New York Irish transplant that had a knack for turning small restaurants into gold mines. He was brought out here seven years ago to protect the golden status of Schwab's. He resisted at first, telling the owners," I am not interested in running a diner!"

Once he saw it and its clientele it was love at first sight. Sam ran the place with smooth discretion, excellent management, and an ongoing sexual fling with Dotty on the side.

"Pure fun sex. Nothing more and nothing less. It was there when I wanted it, however I wanted it," he told his pals back in New York.

Dotty was glad to oblige as she was simply turned on by having someone whose handsomeness she thought was out of reach for a homely woman like her. She was always up for a steamy hot romp most mornings. They met in the kitchen to kick the day off prior to the rest of the staff's arrival. The naughty sacredness of it all thrilled her to no end. The initial guilt took a back seat after indulging in the first round of screaming hot sex. Five years later, she still tingled all over when he pulled her into the kitchen.

One morning as Sam was unlocking the front door to Schwab's, Dotty sneaked up behind him, leaned over his shoulder, and dispatched, "Give me everything in your right front pocket, and I mean EVERYTHING!" Whispering in a raspy low voice.

"Jesus, Dotty! You scared the shit out of me and got me excited all at the same time! Good morning to you too! Look, please be careful, don't stand so close out here on the street. You never know who might drive by. It's a risk neither of us can afford to take. You do still remember that you are married don't you? And that I have a new girlfriend?"

"Mr. O'Brien, I just couldn't help myself after seeing your handsome face." Replying in her best pretense at being sexy.

Sam had reason to worry. He had a new love in his life and was preparing to break off the "special friendship" he'd carried on with Dotty over the years. Her name was Vivien.

"I've got to figure out a way to delicately return the friendship back to a professional one. I just hope she doesn't blow this out of proportion. She is, after all, married. Maybe I can use that angle."

"Hey, Dotty, listen, I am just not comfortable with this any longer, you being married and all. I think we oughta stop this and keep our working friendship on the up and up. Ok?"

"Yeah, that's it. Then, I'll let her know about Viv. The woman I intend to marry."

Chapter Six

TEAM SCHWAB'S

Breakfast has always been a time in Hollywood where deals are made. A vital role Schwab's has worked to its advantage for decades. It used this niche to garner a stable of intriguing regulars of the famous and not so famous.

Everyone, including hustlers, from both the street and the studios, to some of the biggest stars on the screen can be found at iconic Schwab's.

Hollywood is a working town. A town that rises predawn and, in most cases, is in full swing by sunrise.

The world's fantasy factory is busy bringing creative imagination to life while most of the world is still snoozing. Contrary to the famous image of Hollywood being a late late-night, Red Carpet, partying town, this couldn't be farther from the truth.

There is an infrastructure in Hollywood that supports the fantasy machine the world craves. To rule supreme as the creative entertainment capital of the planet takes disciplined professionalism, something Hollywood has maintained since the beginning of moving pictures.

This fusion of cinematic magnetism and hard work encapsulates the magic that delivers the celluloid dreams the world so gleefully scoops up.

The predawn hours in Hollywood are almost mystical. These are the moments that give true voyeurs a chance to enjoy a special view of the city that can only be experienced at these hours. Its wide-open boulevards with little or no traffic sway through sexy neighborhoods with seductive aromas of blooming jasmine gyrating through the air. A quiet aura blankets the city as the lustful moon bows gracefully while exiting the stage, thus allowing the entrance of the dawn's soft sunrise. Glamour town's act one, scene one readies for action.

Movie stars descend gracefully from their villas in mountain-top neighborhoods with names such as Mt. Olympus, Bel-Air, Hollywood Hills, Hancock Park, or Beverly Hills (above Santa Monica Boulevard) through the empty boulevards in their expensive, sleek chariots...limousines, Cadillacs, Jaguars, Bentleys, Mercedes, the list goes on. These are lands where only the rich, famous, beautiful, and seemingly ageless reside.

These neighborhoods might as well be the location of the mythical Mt. Olympus, home of the Greek Gods as far as the regular folks are concerned. Or as the local working class refer to them, "where the hoity-toity of the uppity ups live."

"Don't you dare think you can just go driving around up there! You will be pulled over before you can make it to the first stop sign!" a gardener warned one of his friends who told him he'd like to go sightseeing there someday.

It was as if the stars competed for the few glances of a sacred audience or lone human being stirring on the street, usually a homeless person pushing their life possessions down the street in a shopping cart.

Should you ever find yourself out at this hour, in the early morning, on the Sunset Strip, you might witness one of those beautiful machines pulling over to the curb, lowering its deeply tinted windows, as a forearm reaches out to a poor soul while extending a fist full of U.S. greenbacks.

"Here, please buy yourself some breakfast and clothes," the mystery Star offers while most likely on their way to Schwab's or the studio.

"Why thank you, sir, and God bless you!" the homeless woman, humbled and grateful, replies.

They do this for many reasons. Some out of love and sympathy for humanity, and others out of a haunting fear that in the struggle of life and success in this town, that unfortunate soul could have very well been them. Or, perhaps, could be... someday.

For a "City State" like Hollywood, whose very existence is about creating change, many here prefer and protect certain traditions, Schwab's being one of them.

Dotty had been a central figure in ensuring that Schwab's was "on set" and ready for action each morning. The Schwab's team's performance had become well oiled and delivered like clock work every morning. Dotty and Sam O'Brien were the first to arrive, then Jacques, and finally the cook staff.

"Bonjour, Mademoiselle! You look stunning this morning as usual," Jacques greeted his early arrivals. One phrase of many in his repertoire that he used frequently when practicing his presentation in front of the mirror. His cat had acquired the custom of leaving the room when he saw him approach the mirror. The cat rose to its feet and slowly eased out of the room as if to say, "Please, not again." It continued to do so every time he used that phrase.

Jacques was fond of saying, "I want it to have an effect." And it did. His tips rivaled everyone's inside the diner.

He had a plan. Some people looked down on his position as just that of a valet, yet Jacques saw an opportunity to meet some of the power players of this town. This was a stepping stone in his well orchestrated plan to success. His infusion of

French charm had made him a valuable part of the team at Schwab's. His first step had worked.

A charming man from Nice, France, he'd overstayed his vacation visa about five and half years ago. He soon learned American women had a weakness for an authentic French accent and he used his savoir-faire effectively.

"I want to make a small fortune and return home to my beloved South of France and buy a winery. I am determined not to leave without success in hand," he often told Dotty. He also wanted a part of the movie industry and logged his contacts for future use.

Dotty had a deal for him that could help make his dream come true.

Chapter Seven

SHERMAN OAKS

"It was a Monday, around 9 a.m., I remember it because I was just leaving for a 9:30 appointment with my agent down the street. In walks this tall, well-dressed, well-groomed silver-haired man in an expertly tailored, dark-gray suit. First time I'd ever seen him at Schwab's. I immediately noticed him because of his good taste in expensive clothing. The gentleman took a seat at the counter and appeared to focused his attention on Dotty," Deeves explained to Detective Rocco Goldman.

He wasn't the only one that had taken notice of the man. The Tripartite, forever vigilant for good looking men, were immediately on alert and commenced close observation of what Irene deemed "50 something eye candy."

"Girls, we are going to have to flip for this one!" Natasha exhaled.

"I hate to hurt your feelings, but he's mine. He couldn't take his eyes off my legs when he came in," Bragged Maria-Angela.

"Was he just trying not to trip over them? God knows, you threw it in front of him fast enough!" Natasha replied.

"Right, you just didn't see him walking past. The woman who can spot a good looking fly on the wall," Piped Irene.

"From the looks of it, he sure is eying Dotty up for some reason. One thing we can all agree on, it sure ain't because of her beauty!" Maria-Angela announced.

"Catty this morning ain't we!" Said Natasha. The three women burst out in laughter amongst themselves.

It was odd how the man paid such focused attention to Dotty, especially when she wasn't looking.

"Did you see that?" Asked Irene.

"What?" Asked Natasha.

"Him trying to steal the spoon Dotty put down for his coffee. He pulled a handkerchief out of his pocket to pick up the spoon, then quickly put it down after Dotty turned to face him!" Irene replied.

"Jesus, I hope she doesn't have some kind of disease and he's from the Health Department," Says Irene with real concern.

"You think he might be after her fingerprints?" Natasha suspiciously adds.

"Should we say something to Dotty?" Asks Irene

"Hell no! Not after what she might be doing to us," Maria-Angela states.

"Just keep an eye on him from now on whenever he comes in. Don't let him catch you looking at him for too long," advised Irene.

Michael Deeves had also noticed the odd behavior of the well-dressed stranger, along with his intense observation of Dotty. It appeared to make the man uncomfortable whenever another customer popped in and took a seat next to him. He would abruptly grab his check, pay, and leave in a hurry.

The strange man continued to show up for the next few weeks. Dotty didn't think the small talk he engaged her with was anything out of the ordinary, but he did ask quite a few personal questions.

"Where were you born? Where were your parents born? Are they still alive? Any children?"

She took it as chit chat. But the man was very coy about his background.

"Just stopping in for a bit to eat" was his standard reply. Never offering up any details about his professional background.

In retrospect, she regretted having told him that she had been adopted. Which, strangely enough, he seemed to pay great detail to.

"Have you ever tried to locate your birth parents? Do you know anything about them?" he asked.

That's when Dotty clammed up.

"What are you? Some kind of insurance agent or something?" she had jokingly asked. The point had been made. The conversation made her feel a certain amount of nervousness around him. From that point on, Dotty took her friendliness down a notch or two towards the mysterious customer.

Upon his last visit the entire group of morning regulars took notice when Dotty yelled out at him across the diner, "Drop the coffee cup right there at the door, sir! They're not free ya know!" Yelling like a diner cop!

"Sorry … just forgot. Your coffee's so good!" he replied on his way out the door.

The whole place thought he was up to no good. He never offered any information about himself to anyone.

"Who's your new friend Dotty?" Michael asked.

"No idea. He just started dropping in a few weeks ago. Seems like a nice enough man, if he would only stop asking so many personal questions and taking my coffee cups," she nonchalantly replied.

Her intuition told her differently. She had also watched him watching her through the reflection of the stainless steel appliances behind the counter area.

"What the hell was he staring at me for?" Now a bit worried.

"I hope he's not a reporter … especially from a tabloid. I do not need, nor will I tolerate, competition on my own turf!" Thinking to herself with an air of defiance.

"I'll keep an eye on him from now on out."

Then, out of the blue, he just stopped coming in. Poof! Gone as strangely as when he first appeared.

Chapter Eight

THE HOUSE

The day before her murder, Dotty had phoned Ralph with the good news.

She had taken her occasional drive home from work through Sherman Oaks, always on the lookout for her dream house.

"Oh my! Yes! That is the one! They must have just put the For Sale sign up yesterday."

Pulling over at breakneck speed, she jotted down the number of the Realtor listed on the sign. Hoping that she had finally found her white picket fenced colonial at last.

"I've got the money and now is the time to pounce! I want it!." She'd made up her mind even before seeing the interior of the house. She rang Ralph immediately on the cell phone and announced, "Honey, we're moving!"

"What?"

"I've found the house of my dreams and I am going to talk to the agent today. I'll fill you in on the rest this evening. I'm so excited! Love you!" Click. Hanging up on Ralph before he could get a word in.

"I don't care how much it is!" she thought. "I'm sure I can swing it."

"In cash if I have to."

Dotty made the call to the agent and set up the appointment. The asking price was $1.2 million.

"Is that all they are asking? I want you to understand something. I am a very serious buyer. Do not sell that house until I've seen it, please. Thank you!" That felt damn good to say. "Is that all they are asking? Over a million dollars!" She laughed to herself. Years ago that would have been nothing more than a fantasy. Not anymore. She had more than enough to buy the house, in cash if she wanted to.

"Sweet Jesus, thank you, thank you, thank you!" Sweet Jesus would hardly have helped a conniving antichrist like Dotty Henderson. A woman who had spent years of selling people's private information that had destroyed many of their personal and professional lives.

It was blasphemy for her to even utter the name of Jesus. It was, however, convenient for her to pretend that she was still a good person with morals and ethics. In reality, the only God she truly believed in was a green one called "The Dollar."

"I love the driveway, the fence, huge windows, the yard is wonderful too, with the ivy over the doorway! It's just like the one in my dreams. I have to have this house. I just have to!"

"But Mrs. Henderson, you haven't even seen the inside. It's in excellent condition. The family is selling because of a job transfer. Shall we take a tour of the inside?" pleaded the Realtor.

"That'll be fine. I love it. I'm pretty sure this is...the one!"

Stepping through the doorway onto perfectly maintained, wide-planked, dark wood flooring, they entered the beautiful colonial and faced a rich, circular, mahogany double staircase. It was beyond Dotty's wildest dreams, and far more elegant. She was like a kid in a candy store. There was a medium-sized crystal chandelier hanging above the foyer in the middle of the staircase. Dotty looked up and stared at the twinkling lights as if in her mind she had been transported into another world.

"I want this house. When can they be out?"

"That can be negotiated. I think they are flexible," the Realtor nervously replied.

"I'd like to close the deal as quickly as possible. Can you handle that?" she demanded, as if she had traveled this route many times before.

"What bank will you be using for financing?" queried the Realtor.

"I won't be needing financing. What is the discount for an all cash deal?" Standing in her crisp, server uniform with one hand propped on her hip.

"Uh, well, let's see, um. I can certainly let you know tomorrow?" A hesitant reply as she discreetly looked Dotty over from toe to head.

"This afternoon or evening is preferred. Thank you for your time and my beautiful new home!" Stepping into the new role as the demanding, rich, waitress bitch.

With that, Dotty practically danced her way to the car. Leaving the Realtor standing with her mouth half open not knowing how to respond.

That evening, she shared with Ralph the details of the house.

"Where did you get that kind of money?" he asked, confused.

"I've saved every penny I could get my hand on. And, I've been doing some secret investing in the stock market. I wanted to surprise you, honey!"

"Well, shocked as hell is more like it! I'm not sure if I understand all of this?" He didn't know whether to be happy, angry, or suspicious. What else was she hiding?

Chapter Nine

THE HENDERSONS

The Hendersons moved into their new home as quickly as they could. Dotty was beside herself with happiness and her new found self importance. Here she was, living in her beloved Sherman Oaks, on the street of her dreams, in the house of her dreams.

She was relentless in furnishing it in just the right order. Her general personality had become easygoing, lighthearted, and relaxed. Nothing seemed to bother her.

Her co-workers at Schwab's were, to say the least, thrilled for her. Fortunately, they didn't know the method used to gather her blood money for the purchase.

She had even begun to convince herself that she could dispense with those deep-seated feelings of inferiority.

"I am one of them. A resident of Sherman Oaks. Living in a beautiful home with beautiful furnishings."

One morning while standing outside taking in the beautiful morning air she was greeted by a neighbor.

"Hello! You must be my new neighbor? I'm Marie Cordair, pleasure to meet you!"

"Dotty Henderson, please to meet you, Marie."

"Where'd you move from? Here in L.A?"

"Yes." Dotty hesitated. :Burbank," she said while scanning her neighbor's face for any reaction to it's solidly working-class background.

"Oh, that's nice. Burbank uh, you must be in the film industry too." A natural assumption reflecting the large number of many major film studios located there. Along with anyone who could afford Sherman Oaks' housing prices.

"No, the restaurant business. Just lived there." She just couldn't bring herself to tell the woman she as a waitress at Schwab's. Not here, not in her new Sherman Oaks neighborhood. Making a mental note that she wasn't talking to her old Burbank neighbor, Doris, the mechanic's wife.

"I'm a Director...TV," the friendly neighbor offered.

"Wonderful. Nice meeting you. I'm running a little late. Let's chat another time!" Panicking at the thought of the woman asking which restaurant, along with, "Is it yours?"

"Hell, what am I gonna tell her, 'So, you're a TV director, how fabulous. I'm a waitress at Schwab's over in Hollywood. I'm fucking the boss just because he's handsome and I steal gossip to sell to cheap tabloids. Oh, by the way, the information I sell usually destroys people's marriages and careers. I'm only ashamed when it affects my issues of self-esteem.'" Thinking aloud to herself while loading the washer.

"Or, 'I'm a ruthless bitch who probably caused a young actress to commit suicide when I sold the gossip to a tabloid about her lesbian lover that just happened to be the local female news anchor.'"

"They would have found out anyway. It wasn't really my fault. Look, it's a dog eat cat world. I know what struggling is all about and I don't intend to participate in it my whole life. Anyway, I'm just as good as anyone else in Sherman Oaks now. I own land here!" Trying in vain to justify her odious sense of ethics.

Her confused world was of her own making. In reality, few, if any, successful movie industry artists or executives looked down on anyone working a regular job. Why? Because 99% of them once worked them.

Dotty's perceived class separation was all in her twisted way of thinking. More than likely, her TV director neighbor would have found it fascinating and given the two of them common ground since the director had worked her way through college as a waitress.

Sadly, Dotty felt inadequate because of her personal ethics in life more than her lack of material wealth.

"I gotta find me a deal that's gonna end the Schwab's chapter once and for all. When I do, I'll still sneak over the hill for regular visits with Sam. Can't leave that part behind in my new life." That thought put a smile on her cheating face. Deep down inside, she kind of liked being a cheat at times, it fit right into her thrill-seeking, "cash for gossip" routine.

Her time spent in the beautiful Sherman Oaks home of her dreams wouldn't be long.

Chapter Ten

LIFE AT SCHWAB'S

Once established at Schwab's, Dotty appeared to be the calming force that so many of her regulars sought in the swirling, glamorous, surreal life of Hollywood.

They loved the tradition that the diner offered, along the seemingly rock solid-like force of sweet Dotty.

She had been a participant in this Hollywood routine for 24 years as a dedicated waitress, having landed the sought after position right out of high school. It had been good to her, and it filled her days with loads of excitement many working women would kill for.

"I've never become blasé about the famous people I serve, no matter how many times they've come in."

Her options had been limited growing up and she was thankful for the opportunity Schwab's had provided.

"It may just be waitressing to some, but I have met so many stars and powerful people over the years I can't count half of them," she often told her old Burbank neighbor, Doris.

Schwab's Diner was a daily stop for many of the folks in the movie industry. Located in the center of Hollywood at the intersection of Sunset and Vine, it was almost dead center for multiple movie and TV studios, and the chic neighborhoods of Hancock Park, West Hollywood, or the Hollywood Hills.

A convenient stop for those grabbing a bite of breakfast, coffee, or lunch. Prior to the brutal murder, breakfast at Schwab's had provided a stable social hour as the crossroads of Hollywood. These regulars would be at the center of the murder investigation.

It was a veritable who's who from every walk of life.

It was Monday morning and Ms. Victoria Steele, CEO of American International Film Studio, left her palatial Hancock Park villa. Gliding down her wide, lush driveway onto the quiet street that turns towards Hollywood, heading in the same direction taken every morning as she headed out for breakfast. She was seeking her first taste of real life before commanding the film sets of her studio. Her job required her to create glamorous dreams full of intrigue, similar to the thread that ran through her real life. Her routine stop before the office gave her a tangible chance to stay in touch with the feel of the street and people outside the cocoon of the Hollywood wealth. A vital resource when green lighting contemporary, multi-million dollar movie projects. Her societal lab was Schwab's.

With her white, red, black, and gold Hermes scarf fashioned tightly wrapped around her head and neck, ala late 1950's-60's chic, along with the obligatory large black Chanel sunglasses, she made one last mirror check.

The look was befitting a stunning Hollywood beauty in a sleek white Jaguar convertible. The fresh morning air with just the right amount of chill was invigorating.

"How lucky we are to live here," she thought as she flipped her collar up to embrace her neck and face with the feel of smooth, soft, luxurious tan cashmere.

"We have the beach, mountains, and desert all within a few hours drive from the city. Oh, how I love this town!"

Today would be one of those days when she discovered just how lucky she can be.

Victoria was disarming to many of the powerful men she struck deals with in her position as CEO of one of the biggest and most successful film studios in Hollywood. She had led the studio to record profits over the past two years. She was also as beautiful as many of the female stars that brought her movies to life. This belied her accomplishments when dealing with powerful men she frequently battled in this industry.

Fresh from a disappointing romance with one of Hollywood's leading men, she drove steady and assuredly north on Vine towards Sunset as she mentally dissected her breakup. Rarely doubting herself and always fully prepared, she had learned the film business inside out. She made her way from young intern to studio CEO in less than 12 years of relentless drive and a Stanford MBA that prepared her for the shrewd risks that success in this business demanded. It took dedication, and at present, and empty heart. It took the sacrifice of having to settle for the crowd she was most familiar with for her pool of lovers and potential husbands: stars and powerful titans of the film industry. Not bad, but not quite the steady, passionate rock she'd been hoping for in life. Her last break up reminded her of that.

Thinking to herself, "If I have to hear, 'Imagine what we could create together with my talent and your power,' one more time."

* * *

Recent Hollywood arrival, Cino Salvaggio, stepped out onto his balcony and sipped his morning coffee while taking in the expansive view of the city. His new apartment was located at the beautifully preserved Chateau du Fleur.

Legendary director, Mr. Cecil B. DeMille had done an excellent job when he built this French chateau style apartment building for his fledgling stars back in the 1920's. Perfectly positioned atop the Franklin Hills, it provided a commanding view of central Hollywood.

All the more to remind his up and coming new stars of the kingdom they must conquer.

"This would cost a fortune back in Rome. If it could even be found. Something like this on the market would be rare indeed." He loved his new place and his new city.

"I am in Hollywood, and I will create a beautiful life here." As he admired the city laid out below him.

"I still believe in chasing my dreams and I will forever chase love until I find it." Allowing his romantic soul to remind him of why he was in this new town, and starting a new life.

Legend dictates that even the simple task of going to work in movie town can sometimes alter your life forever. These unknown detours are embraced. A shared characteristic that appeared to make them thrive on life's surprises, be they bad or good, obstacles had a way of honing their cleverness."Mio Bella Roma." Thinking of his life back in Rome. Where beauty was simply a fact of everyday life, from its buildings, people, food, language, and most importantly the love and passion that ruled daily life.

Cino had known Rome and Italy well. He decided that he should explore the world a bit beyond Europe before settling down for good. He chose California for his next adventure, Hollywood to be exact. Having grown up with its films, he wanted to see its beautiful beaches and way of life. He also wanted to get as far away as possible from his ex-lover, the beautiful but obsessive young countess that refused to comprehend that she couldn't buy his love. But, that was the past.

"Spero!" I hope!

Besides, with his expert skills as specialist on exotic Italian and English automobiles, he needed to be in a city that could afford them. Hollywood was by far the largest consumer market of expensive European imports in the world. The wealth here is "spectacular," he thought.

Cino was a Ferrari/Jaguar specialist. He felt that it was irrelevant that he had rugged, classic Roman handsomeness. Even if his undeniable, cocky, sexual charisma could have made him an instant star.

He never entertained those kinds of ambitions. Keenly aware that he had the goods, should he ever want to go that route.

He was a perfectionist in all of his undertakings. His passion didn't allow him to just master it, his devotion required him to become one with whatever it was.

The nickname "Grande Ferrari," the Big Ferrari, wasn't just because of his expert skill when working on the handcrafted, Italian motor stallion.

At 35, and fully aware of his prowess, he quite enjoyed putting it on display at times. The exhibitionism in him was just a notch above the normal attitude of the men of Italy. Which normally ran higher than most others.

His appreciation for beauty was not just limited to the curves and lines of buildings. Cino Salvaggio took great pleasure in running his hands along the voluptuous curves of his beloved Ferrari's and Jaguars, amongst other passionate objects in his life.

He sported a wild mass of long, black, curly hair, shaped by a face centered by a perfect Roman nose, stationed atop a 6'1", 195-pound frame of lean, tanned muscle. A body that was tuned to near male perfection.

He was far from conceited, but he was clearly aware of his gifts. He knew it, women knew it, and quite a few men as well. The combo of Italian charm, intelligence, and a sincere demeanor was an intoxicating, and dangerous potion for any female he set his eyes on.

That morning, he was headed out for "una buona colazione" at a place he'd walked past on his walk to work at Hollywood Ferrari/Jaguar.

"Con il nome di Schwab's." With the name of Schwab's.

Before heading out, he grabbed a parting glance that so vividly displayed the beautiful city beneath his windows.

"E bella questa citta! Mi piace un sacco! How beautiful this city is! I love it!" he thought to himself in Italian with an excited smile on his face. He was quickly falling in love with Los Angeles.

Chapter Eleven

TRIPARTITE/VICTORIA

Victoria Steele pulled in front of Schwab's and shifted her sleek Jaguar into park. Jacques hand was on the car handle before the car had completely stopped.

"Bonjour, Ms. Steele! It is a pleasure to see you this morning!"

"Good morning, Jacques! Thank you."

She gracefully entered Schwab's as demurely as once can when dressed so noticeably chic. Finding her way to her favorite spot at the counter, two seats from the far end of the wall. A spot she had enjoyed, undisturbed, for several years now.

Removing her coat and scarf, she seated herself and laid out her trade papers onto the counter next to a fresh cup of piping hot coffee.

Dotty has pre-poured with perfect timing, anticipating Victoria's arrival. This kind of superior service was simply expected there. It was the reputation they had built.

As soon as Ms. Steele was seated, her food was placed in front of her. Her standard meal consisted of multi grain toast, slightly burned and buttered, and fresh fruit, California grown organic, only.

"Ms. Steele, good morning! You are looking as beautiful as ever."

"Thank you, Dotty, hope you had a lovely weekend, the coffee is delish." Victoria was friendly, yet not too informal. As head of a powerful film studio, one had to be careful.

She settled down with the trades after looking around and finding everything rolling along as it always had at this hour.

Cino headed down Cherokee Avenue towards Hollywood Boulevard, then cutting over to Vine and Sunset.

"This is fantastic; I can walk to work in "dieci minuti!"

This morning, however, he had allotted enough time for a breakfast detour.

Strutting in his white work jumpsuit with red Ferrari/Jaguar printed on the back in bold letters gave him an extra bounce in his stride. It fit him to a "T", tight in all the right places. After all, as a single Italian man in a new city, he was required to make some kind of effort to announce to the beautiful woman that he had arrived. The jumpsuit did just the trick, it put the merchandise on display, just enough. Any tighter in the front and it might cause a red alert and have them following him home.

"I must maintain some respectability…but not too much!"

He smiled devilishly to himself.

* * *

Rocco Goldman swung through the door to Schwab's, he was a local Hollywood PD finishing up his all-nighter.

"Hey, Dot, Sam! I'm starving! How bout the works this morning, throw some extra bacon on there!"

"Coming right up, handsome."

Entering Schwab's, a minute after Rocco, was Cino Salvaggio in all his gorgeous, Italian glory. The hustle and bustle of the restaurant almost fell completely still. Out of embarrassment the murmur of chat returned.

Cino entered, looked around, and walked past three empty seats at the counter. Without hesitation, he took the seat directly next to Victoria.

She became completely aware of his presence, but did not look up beyond her paper. Cino glanced respectfully at her, wanted to say hello, but did not want to intrude.

He knew that she was aware of him, as he could see her blushing face. The feeling was mutual. He was instantly attracted to her.

Victoria was at first taken aback that a stranger had chosen the seat next to her in lieu of all the other empty seats farther away. Nor was she interested in an early morning chat. She was curious though, and stole a glance of the stranger with her peripheral vision. In order not to appear rude, she allowed herself to extend a fleeting, "Good morning," and immediately felt overwhelmed by a dose of his intoxicating sexiness.

Cino turned to stare directly into her eyes.

"Ah, buongiorno to you too!" He took in the reflection of light on her beautiful shiny hair and the faint, sweet smell of her perfume.

In just those few seconds, he had glimpsed them together at dinner with candlelight glowing on her beautiful face.

Victoria quickly turned her head. She had felt a shock wave of attraction hit her like the summer heat of August after you leave a chilled, air-conditioned building.

"Like when the sweaty, humid heat causes your skin to instantly begin to moisten and glisten," she would later confide in a friend.

"Dear God! He is the most beautiful man on earth!" Secretly thinking to herself.

"I'm blushing. I can't embarrass myself like this, everyone in the restaurant must be staring at the two of us. Pull yourself together, Victoria, and stop letting your hormones run wild like a silly school girl!"

"Dotty, is the air on? It's a bit warm, don't you think?" she pleaded without looking in the direction of Cino.

Cino thought that it was impolite for her to just say "hello," and then ignore him.

"Yes, it is getting a little hot in here. I'll turn up the air a bit," Dotty replied with a smirky half smile.

"Not very gracious for a lady of her caliber," he thought, less than he had expected from such a stunning beauty who one would assume had been raised with etiquette and charm. Rudeness was not tolerated by him, from any woman. He turned his head forward and focused on his meal, not speaking another word nor glancing in her direction.

"He's not interested in me. He must be married, got a girlfriend, or gay. That's it, he must be gay! No straight man this handsome would ignore a pretty female, like myself, unless he's gay." Thinking to herself. That usually helped massage her beauty queen ego.

"Gosh, what if he is straight and I've blown it. Was I rude?" Second guessing her actions.

Cino finished his meal and immediately paid his bill as Dotty stood staring at his handsome face.

"New to Schwab's"

"Si. I've just moved from Rome, Italia."

"Such lovely, beautiful men…err, people! Welcome to Hollywood and Schwab's. I hope we see more of you, I'm Dotty."

"Thank you Dotty, molto gentile."

He kept his conversation short and polite, then rose to leave without one additional word or nod in the direction of the beauty that had captured his eye and perhaps his heart, moments earlier.

As he turned and headed for the door, Victoria nonchalantly glanced over her shoulder and caught the large, bold, red lettering on the back of his jumpsuit, "Hollywood Ferrari/ Jaguar."

Replaying the experience over to herself she thought, "I won't be this timid tomorrow. I'll let him know in my own sweet way that I find him attractive. One way or another, I'll know if there is any chemistry. I mean, he did choose to sit next to me when there were other seats available." Dissecting the thrill, doubt, and confidence of a possible new romance.

"I think I am excited!"

It was a rare episode in her jaded world. She had just ended her long-term relationship with super star Fox Wyatt, recently voted sexiest man alive by Peeps magazine, whom she thought was marriage potential, until he was caught by paparazzi with a slew of strippers in a cheap motel out in the Valley.

She was in no hurry to dive in again. But, this guy had a good energy vibe, not to mention he was physically quite the male specimen. She felt compelled to learn more about him.

* * *

Not one millisecond of this action had escaped the three longtime friends who had been Schwab's pals for over five years. Maria-Angela Cortez debated with the other two women, Irene West and Natasha Komistaya, if she should "trip him or take the seat next to him." All three were in agreement that the ultimate specimen of maleness had just walked in, and none were too happy that "Ms. Executive Stuck-up" had struck gold with him…or had she?

"Perhaps he prefers women with warm blood in their veins," was Irene's scathing comment.

"And Ms. Movie Studio clearly has ice water for blood," snapped Natasha Komistaya in her driest, cold-hearted Russian accent.

These women were known as the "Tripartite." All former, but still ready for the call, performers in show biz.

They met at Schwab's promptly every morning at 7:15 a.m. for coffee and to dish the dirt about their famous employers, along with the latest tabloid gossip. Same time, same table, without fail, rain or shine. The kind of dirt that comes directly from the source, "no fake bull shit" for these women. They dealt with the real, live, nuclear material—their employers.

Irene was an actress with a list of B movies and irregular soap opera credits that had provided her a suitable amount of funds to live on comfortably. Until, that is, she was swindled, along with many others from Hollywood, far richer, of hundreds of millions of dollars by a major Wall Street Ponzi Scheme criminal.

"That slimy son of a bitch made off with all my cash and left me nearly penniless. If only I could get my chance to burn that motherfucker with some hot frying grease straight to the face! I know I shouldn't think like that, Lord, save me from these horrible thoughts. After I burn his thieving ass!" She clung to the timeless advice that her mother use to live by. "You reap what you sow, Irene," her mother always told her.

"I only hope he reaps it over and over till hell freezes over" was her reply.

Their daily ritual had been in play every weekday morning for the last five years.

The long road of show business can be cold, lonely, and woefully regretful. Artists lead a difficult life of rejection, hit or miss, or just plain damn good luck. These three women artists were old pros who had had not quite as much good luck as the bad kind. They were, however, tough, practical survivors.

Irene West took a housekeeper's job to survive! Mind you, not just "any" housekeeper's position. She worked for powerful studio head, Breeze Rainbolt, a kind no nonsense man, recently divorced for the third time.

Ms. West was smart and an obsessive stock market investor with an uncontrollable penchant for gossip and finance. Her secret to running a successful household, of which she swore by, was listening to the business channel in every room while cleaning.

"It takes me to my Zen spot," she stated while comparing notes with her two friends.

Her employer, Breeze Rainbolt, had just been charged with the murder of his last wife's lover. A scandal that filled the front pages of the Hollywood Examiner and others on a daily basis. It was true that he'd threatened to kill her, her lover, and his entire family…after he'd make him watch as he burned his wife alive in front of him with his sliced off lollipop stuffed in her mouth since she was so hungry for it. All caught on a cell phone recording. Luckily it was dismissed, as it was illegally recorded, and as such, it was inadmissible in the state of California.

"Thankfully, California takes its citizens' privacy seriously," he stated to the press.

"I deeply loved my wife and was simply reacting to an uncontrollable fit of rage after walking in on her and her lover… in my bed."

The rest of the story was, as Irene shared with her two gossip sisters, "He overheard her declaring how much she loved performing "spin the potter's wheel" on her lover's magic stick with her tongue and hands. While her naked, engorged lover laid back against the headboard."

A trick Breeze was led to believe was only shared between the two of them.

He'd sworn he had only beat the hell out of the guy, as he fled the house, then threw her out behind him without a stitch of clothes on. Dramatic, yes, but he never murdered the guy who showed up dead in the Hollywood Reservoir a week later.

Irene loved every juicy minute of it. She stood by his side through it all, never flinching in her belief of his innocence. Call it women's intuition. Deep down inside, she just knew Mr. Rainbolt wouldn't kill a fly. He hated to even see plants die, let alone humans.

Breeze Rainbolt was vindicated when the investigation revealed that Mrs. Rainbolt was in fact the murderer, upon discovering, two days later, her lover with another woman.

"Karma is a boomerang," as they say in the canyons of New Age Malibu.

Mr. Rainbolt was released back into the open arms of Hollywood in a manner that made one think he had just won Best Picture of the year.

Ms. Irene West now drove a brand new silver Mercedes roadster, complements of her employer. He promised her an audition when the right project came along. Irene helped him believe that his innocence would keep him safe during very dark days.

Former Russian beauty queen Natasha Kamitstaya lived comfortably in her small East West Hollywood bungalow and worked for TV super star Blanche Lane. Ms. Lane was currently the highest paid actor on TV, with three Emmy's under her belt.

Natasha was a singer and dancer who was well on her way to success in Russian entertainment prior to moving to Los Angeles. After the fall of the Soviet Union lawlessness reigned supreme across Russia. It spread like a cancer across the country. Russian criminals became so emboldened that they sought out the successful elements of Russian society with the profitable intention of kidnapping and extortion.

"I had to get out of there or be killed," she told her friend upon arrival in Los Angeles.

The final straw was when she was accosted by thugs after a shopping trip.

"Hey, aren't you Natasha Komistaya? The entertainer from TV?" the thug demanded.

"No! I am not!"

The criminal looked into her eyes while smiling and stated, "We know where you live."

She fled Russia that week and never returned.

Being a successful singer in your native language is one thing, mastering it in another language is quite another. She believed she could do it, and would keep trying. In the meantime, she had to pay the bills. Her savings had lasted a few years after buying a small cottage.

Natasha was fortunate enough to have been personally recommended for the job of running Ms. Lane's household. She had been generously rewarded for her efforts.

The Tripartite third anchor was dancer Maria-Angela Cortez. Ex-Broadway dancer and current controller of household staff to one Ms. Mae Vaught. Yes, that would be the legendary film star Mae Vaught.

She was third generation American and was quick to remind you that she was not by any stretch of the imagination "an illegal alien" just because her last name ended in "ez."

Her legs were as fit and ready as they were during her last show on Broadway 5 1/2 years earlier. Maria-Angela kept them ready by dancing all day while taking care of business at work. She was determined to be ready when and if that next call or audition came. Her tap shoes hung by the door to remind her every day what her first mission was as an artist.

She was also the flirt of the trio, known to fallen in love at least twice in one breakfast setting.

"Remember, I was the first one to 'spot' the heat between Dotty and Sam. It takes one to know one!" Laughing while reminding the girls.

"It was the way they tried to ignore each other while working. I am clever that way."

"The love connection is my field of PhD and don't either of you forget it." As the other two women howled.

"I have only had bad luck with men lately because they only want me for my legs!"

And indeed, what a set of legs she did have. Long, caramel, Tina Turner legs, one of which she made sure was "accidentally" extended while sitting at the edge of a table every morning.

"My muscles need to stretch or they will get violent!" she told her giggling friends at the table.

"Honey, violence is what men want from those legs of yours!" stated Irene. All three let go of a backstage belly roll!

"I've tried so hard to tame them, but they just can't be tamed."

The three of them were in the thick of it all and used their morning meeting to pump up the volume of energy between them before heading out for work.

* * *

Victoria thought about the dark, handsome stranger in the "race car driver overalls" all day that day. In fact she couldn't think of anything else. Once at home, she analyzed the interaction that had occurred between the two of them. Playing it out over and over in her head, she hoped she had not been too distant towards him. She concluded that she could make it up to him in the morning by being extra friendly and sweet. Surely he would show up again, he seemed to like the place.

"Oh, damn, what if he doesn't come in? What if I have just ignored what could have been the sexiest man I have ever met?"

"What an idiot I am! 'Always keeping the wall up for protection!' Ok…get a grip on yourself, he'll show again. I am sure he will. I can feel it. I hope?"

Victoria had to self-consciously behave in a normal manner the following morning. It was an attempt to appear normal while fighting to contain her excitement. She had selected the sexiest business suit she could find in her vast clothing when getting prepared for work that morning. Hoping to impress her "new man," who she had not even formally met. Admitting to herself that there was no denying the intense attraction that she felt between them. So brief, yet so powerful.

"I can't ever remember being so enamored and affected by meeting a man as I have been with Mr. Sexy Ferrari."

The following morning, the Tripartite were all wearing bright red and pink glossy lipstick and looking particularly fashionable in their form-fitting blouses and sweaters. No doubt hoping to get their chance to catch the eye of the Ferrari stallion.

"Ms. Executive Stuck-up" had her work cut out for her with the local competition.

Victoria took her usual seat.

"Hi, Dotty! Isn't beautiful outside this morning!" she exclaimed.

"Good morning, Miss. Steele, yes it is beautiful today, and so are you. Love that suit, it looks wonderful on you. Better be careful, you might catch some big Italian's eye dressed like that!" Dotty said with a wink and a smile.

"Oh, I don't think so, Dotty." As demurely as she could, worried that all the women, and men for that matter, in the place could tell she was anticipating another chance meeting with Mr. Dark and Handsome that morning.

Victoria went about her routine as usual, with the only exception being that her heart skipped a beat every time the front door swung open. Seven-thirty arrived, nothing...then eight o'clock, then eight-fifteen. He wasn't coming. She had to leave for work as her schedule was packed that morning. Maybe he would show tomorrow. She had to believe there would be a second chance. She just knew there would be.

* * *

"Well, I guess the rich bitch ran the stallion away," lamented Natasha, referring to Victoria.

"No wonder that last movie of hers broke her winning streak. If she casts for movies like she does for dates, she's in big trouble!" Laughing amongst themselves.

"I see ol' Dotty wasted no time getting acquainted with the new "Michelangelo of Hollywood," Maria-Angela added.

"Doesn't she have a husband ... AND Sam?" cracked Irene.

Victoria was anxious, once again, in anticipation of the next morning. She had butterflies in her stomach at thinking about seeing the man from Italy. It had been a brief encounter, but she couldn't stop thinking about him. The way he stared so boldly into her eyes, everything in the blink of a second. She had made up her mind the night before, as a woman of action, that if he failed to show this morning, she had remembered "Hollywood Ferrari/Jaguar" on the back of his overalls.

She hadn't become CEO of a leading film studio by waiting around, wishing for rainbows. She knew when to recognize opportunity. This put Victoria's determination on the front burner. By the time her evening had ended and she crawled into bed, Victoria allowed herself to fantasize for a moment what it would be like to kiss his incredibly handsome face.

"What the hell! Snap out of this nonsense! You don't even know this man and you are already thinking about kissing him!" Lamenting to herself aloud.

With that she flicked the light switch off and tried to sleep, but couldn't get that mass of curly black hair and citrus smell out of her mind. Finally she drifted off to sleep thinking about life in rustic Italy.

Under false pretense; Victoria had a reason for her visit to Hollywood Ferrari/Jaguar. Ms. Steele informed her personal Jaguar consultant that an unusual sound was suddenly emanating from her car.

"I need it looked at immediately please."

Her true intention was to hopefully cross paths "accidentally" with the man that had made her blush so profusely.

While waiting nervously, she heard the PA announcement,

"Cino, please meet Ms. Steele in the lobby for immediate assistance."

Victoria was not certain of his name, but she believed she had overheard him telling Dotty that it was in fact Cino.

"That Dotty, thank goodness for her friendly sweetness, she's helped in ways that she will never know." Reminding herself of the other morning.

Immediately after the announcement the large service doors swung open. Victoria suddenly felt a rush of excitement hit her, then utter and complete disappointment. In walked an older gentleman that could have been her Italian's grandfather, half his size and the farthest away from her "Mr. Italy" that she could have imagined. The older gentleman was heading straight towards her as her shoulders slumped in obvious disappointment, chopping off a full inch of her height as they sank.

"Could I be at the wrong location?" she asked herself as the older man neared her. An accented, deep, hypnotic voice from behind her made her melt like warm chocolate on a hot day spoke to her, "Signorina Steele?"

Startled, she stared as the older gentleman strolled past her. Victoria slowly turned, heart racing from nervousness, excitement, and hope, to face none other than Mr. Cino Salvaggio in all his gloriousness.

"I will extend a far better impression upon him this time around." Thinking to herself.

"Well, hello there!" she said in a feigned surprised greeting.

"What a coincidence running into you again!" she faked and flashed a smile.

"I am sorry; I don't understand? There is an issue with your car, no?" he replied in a coldly formal manner.

"Umm, yes, there is a strange noise coming from the engine. I wanted to investigate it right away," Victoria stumbled.

"I see; shall we take a look?" Cino spoke in a serious tone.

"Yes, of course. May I ask, do you not remember us meeting a few days ago? At Schwab's?" Hesitating while starting to lose her nerve.

In his most defiant attitude, he declared, "You have assuredly mistaken me for someone else as I am quite clear we have never met." Matching the same dry tone she used in her "Good morning" to him the other day.

Victoria, now immensely embarrassed, assumed that he was indeed not interested in her and that she had completely misread his initial intentions.

They proceeded to the car as he asked for her keys. Now, completely rattled, she timidly laid the keys in his large, tan hands. Cino immediately felt a shock wave pulse through him as her soft hand slightly touched his.

After starting the car and hearing nothing out of the ordinary from the engine, just as Cino had suspected, he said "Perhaps we should take it for a drive around the block to gather the feel of it in action?"

"Of course, you are the expert."

"THAT I am."

Victoria went silent and pondered what a fool she had made of herself.

She began to withdraw from the interaction, hoping to regain some level of dignity from her bruised ego.

Cino walked to the passenger side of the sleek convertible and assisted with the passenger door as Ms. Steel eased into the intimate two-seater. He then slid his large frame into the driver's seat and started the engine. They drove off into traffic with an uneasy wall of silence lingering and stinging bewilderment between them. Upon reaching the first stop light, both stared straight ahead in uncomfortable silence.

With a mixture of humility and authority, Cino stated, "Of course I remember you, I haven't been able to stop thinking about you since the moment I laid eyes on you."

It had been apparent to him that there were no issues with the car, long before taking it for a drive. It was also obvious that she had sought him out on a contrived expedition on her behalf to locate him.

"My instincts were spot on from the first time we looked at each other. I felt it," he thought.

There was undeniable tension and chemistry between the two of them mixed with wild expectation, which was finally acknowledged by both. Cino was startled by the sound of a blasting horn behind them as the light had long been green. Although he'd been looking straight ahead, the change of light had gone completely unnoticed. He immediately pulled the car over to the curb.

The intimate pod of the luxurious sports car forced them to look at each other for the first time with open feelings of intense excitement. Cino took his right hand from the car's gear shift and rubbed the outside of his fingers down her smooth left cheek, staring deeply into her eyes for a moment of intense silence.

"May I have dinner with you tonight?"

"I would like that very much," Victoria replied in a hushed voice.

"I'll pick you up. I know a wonderful small Italian place I'd like to share with you." she continued.

"Perfetto. What time?"

"Is 7:30 OK?" she asked.

"Va bene," that's great, replied Cino.

At that very moment, Victoria would later swear she could count each and every long black eyelash languishing around those big dreamy brown eyes.

Cino was swimming in beauty again. He now felt at home in his new Hollywood for the first time since his arrival. He was staring at the kind of beauty his eyes were used to. This was the beginning of a serious story. The kind your gut and tells you, "This is what being human is all about."

It switches on instincts that you never knew even existed, something like you had never encountered in the arena of love.

"Victoria Salvaggio. Umm, I like the sound of that," she thought.

"E cosi comincia!" And so it begins! He smiled to himself.

Chapter Twelve

MICHAEL/MAE

Screenwriter Michael Deeves found all the subtle drama that morning highly entertaining. An expert people watcher, he rarely missed many nuances of human behavior while seated in what could only be referred to as the "bird's eye view." He was definitely the cool, silent type. Forever seeking out the characters who live out their lives in his screenplays, he was an observer of the nth degree.

"I observe my characters from above, almost as if I am in an ethereal floating state while viewing them in action."

"Schwab's is the perfect locale. I have been coming to Schwab's since childhood having first been introduced by my mother on a Saturday shopping trip. It was about a week after watching Sunset Boulevard for the first time," he told a friend.

"There I was, gliding through the doors of Headquarters' as it was known in the movie.

"'Headquarters' being the local Hollywood hangout for the up and coming artists of the movie, music, and literary circles. Based on that movie alone, I expected to walk in and see the joint full of starlets, writers, singers, and deal makers. I settled at the soda fountain with a Coke and hot dog. The only stunning beauty in the place was my mom. Let there be no doubt, had it not been for me and my siblings, she could have had Hollywood at her feet with a face like hers.

"My "office" at Headquarters was a small booth situated in the corner at 2:00 high. It gave me the perfect 360 of the entire place. At mid-way in my career, I have been told that the looks are still there and I have no trouble holding my own with the young starlets, especially when they find out that I am a writer. It certainly doesn't hurt to have a 6' 165-pound lean swimmer's build either.

"Hey, life is about the angles, and I try to work everyone... including the William Holden look-alike with smart looking reading glasses.

"Starlets love the mother and son shopping trip story and I never tire of telling it to their willing ears," he shares with another writing buddy.

"The rotation of characters at Schwab's is where my fascination lies. There is a non stop supply of "gonnebees," who's gonna be somebody, followed by the constant re-supply of "couldabbeens," as in "I could have been somebody.

"It's simply paradise for a writer," he exclaims.

"Just look at all the fluttering going on with these women this morning. All of this over one good looking stranger. They all behaved as if Zeus had walked in looking for a wife!"

Michael was a bit curious himself about the guy in the bright Ferrari overalls. Was he a race car driver?

"A new character for my work, for sure."

He figured he would eventually hear it all from Dotty anyway. Dotty ran a tight ship and knew just about everyone, and everything about everyone, that walked in the door, within 10 minutes. She was friendly that way. These regulars had become a sort of Breakfast Club with the occasional new face to stimulate things.

Deeves started out as an actor. Not just any kind of actor, but a method actor! The kind who bring characters to life via experience. This was a mission that he took very seriously. He had left Hollywood for life experience in New York, Rome, London, and around the world, only to discover that it was all right here in Hollywood, along with perfect weather to boot. This town was one of the most powerful magnets in the world, the possibility of fame and fortune making it irresistible.

As an actor who had had limited luck with stage, film, and TV, he needed to find a way for his characters to come to life when the acting agent wasn't calling. Writing was the answer.

"I had my office and an all-day supply of java from Dotty. No pressure to drink and leave as they had come to realize the value in having the place look filled with the artsy types." Telling a friend.

"How's that Oscar winning screenplay coming?" was Dotty's routine question once a week.

"Just don't you forget poor little ol' Dotty when you hit the jackpot!"

"I won't...I promise. Your coffee is the fuel that has kept the engine going Dotty." Laughing to himself at the thought of catching Dotty sneaking longing glances at Sam. She had no idea that he had walked past the window early one morning before opening and caught a peek of the two of them kissing in the kitchen.

"Hey, whatever floats your boat," he chuckled. Michael was a staunch believer in never "kissing and telling."

* * *

Maria-Angela had interviewed four times for the household position with the movie icon, Mae Vaught. Ms. Vaught offered her the job after a chance meeting at Schwab's during which

Maria-Angela let slip that she secretly danced while doing housework. Ms. Vaught loved it! Informing Maria-Angela, "An artist for an artist, you've got the job as long as you keep dancing!" She's had been counted among the screen legend's few close confidants since.

Legendary film star Mae Vaught exploded onto the Hollywood movie scene in 1944 at the age of 19 by winning the Oscar for Best Actress in A River With No End. Mae brought with her an exotic face, piercing blue-gray eyes, and a fiery persona. Her exquisite etiquette and mysterious past only added to her allure. There was speculation that led many to believe that she was indeed descended from exotic royalty. A rumor that had been cooked up by a tabloid reflecting her Oscar winning film role.

The lead role was that of a half-breed, Indian princess kidnapped and forced to marry a powerful, barbaric white rancher enchanted by her irresistible beauty. So captured by her charm he prevented her escape three times as she attempted to flee down river back to her people. Upon return after the third attempt she decided to stay and fight for her life. The ensuing battle resulted in the untimely death of the arrogant rancher and her eventual control of his fortune. Those who had assisted in her imprisonment and recapture now faced her revenge. The movie was a massive box office hit!

"I've had to fight for everything in my life. From decent film roles to pay. I won more than I lost!" she was fond of saying.

Mae Vaught had held Hollywood at her feet, having reached the pinnacle of box-office power early in her career. She was one of the first actors to demand a percentage of her films in lieu of a straight salary. This shrewd move endowed her with enormous wealth even by Hollywood's standards.

Her life had been shared by two husbands. The first sought a divorce and half her fortune upon discovering that her

"German" ancestry was overshadowed by a much larger percentage of real Cherokee blood... and for icing on the cake, a black grandmother! All of which was barely reflected in her white skin, blue-gray eyes, and envious face, except her incredible cheekbones.

One must remember this was an era of intense racial discrimination. Mae had fried much bigger fish when facing down Hollywood studio heads.

"I demanded a fair share in my highly successful career. They didn't like that. But I won." Relating the story to journalists.

As one of the richest women, or men for that matter, in Hollywood, she would not be deterred or flinch in defense of her reputation and honor...along with the best legal minds a huge fortune could buy. Her sense of fairness fueled her passion to fight injustice.

Having been raised under mixed parentage she understood a smattering of the Cherokee language. Her traitorous first husband, the spoiler, hustler, ex-theatrical agent and seeker of a free fortune, had discovered her secret and verified it by speaking to her one morning in Cherokee.

"Osdasunale." Good morning. He'd spent a week learning the proper pronunciation.

She automatically replied, "Wado," thank you, and quickly realized what he had done.

He used this as a confrontation to blackmail her about her secret past.

A fierce survivor, Mae met the accusation head on by holding a press conference to announce to the world, "It was discovered that I am of mixed Cherokee heritage, and I hope it will not change the love and devotion of my fans. I say this based on the equality of all human kind, so defined in our beloved US Constitution." And she continued on with something about, "All red blooded, decent Americans believe in freedom and justice for all!"

It worked. Months later, upon exiting the court house, when questioned by reporters about her feelings regarding her just-granted divorce, her only reply, as she stopped cold and stared directly into the reporters eyes was, "Lie down with dogs...well, you know the rest."

"I am thrilled to know how devoted my fans are, and to discover that I am OK!" she exclaimed, as she turned for a wave to the cameras before boarding her handcrafted 1938 Bugatti Type 57SC Atlantic en route to her villa in the ultra exclusive Bel-Air section of Hollywood.

The crushing crowd of admirers screamed, "Our Cherokee Princess!"

Mae had secretly taken care of her beloved black grandmother in luxury for years. She was to discover later, that she was not by a long shot, the only mixed blooded American star gracing the silver screen as they fulfilled the dreams of an era and a society full of racism.

"Hell, I am probably the most American of most of America!" she would say with a laugh while talking to Maria-Angela.

Chapter Thirteen

VIC/CINO

Victoria and Cino spent the evening dining in the dim lights of La Luna e Stelle (The Moon and Stars). With only seven tables, the quaint Italian restaurant was one of the more intimate establishments on the Sunset Plaza. Known for it's clientele of stars, it was nearly impossible for the average person to book a table.

Although it was located in West Hollywood, one would have thought it was the Amalfi Coast or Capri from the ambiance and aroma emanating from the kitchen. The food was perfection, the service divine, and the companionship a fantasy come true. The unspoken passion had kidnapped them and threaten to consume them. Cino held her hand from across the table for what seemed like the entire evening. Victoria had challenged herself in a vain attempt of trying to remember if she had ever felt this way about a new romance. A feeling of being consumed by a fog of attraction like she had never felt before.

"I scarcely remember what we had for dinner," she would later relay to Dotty.

"Can I offer you a nightcap at my place?" she asked Cino.

"That would be wonderful, but, I beg you, first, please allow me to share something with you at my home on a special night like this? Then we can go to your place if you like," he pleaded.

Victoria obliged. While driving up the steep hill towards Cino's apartment building in the Franklin Hills, they marveled at the magnificent and enormous full moon. It faced them head-on. It seemed as if they were driving directly into it. The moonlight glowed over the entire neighborhood. It was a full, harvest summer moon, and it sat right smack in the middle of Franklin Avenue as it rose up the hill. The moon sat against the clear night sky full of sparkling stars. Real stars, the kind that took the universe billions of years to create. Ones that have more staying power than all the stars of Hollywood combined.

They arrived at his building, the Chateau du Fleur. Victoria was struck by the awesome beauty of it against the moonlight; it was magical. She felt as if she was staring in one of her movies full of romance.

"No movie could ever be this good," she thought.

Cino opened the door to his apartment and introduced Victoria to a breathtaking, floor to ceiling wall of windows with the lights of Hollywood glimmering in the night sky. It was captivating. His apartment was minimally furnished with just a few pieces of expensive contemporary Italian designed furnishings. Two deep chocolate leather chairs sat in the middle of the windows with a small table separating them as if chaperoning the two amidst the romantic night view.

"Please have a seat. I'll be right back," he offered.

She continued standing, transfixed by the hypnotic view from his window, of the city that unfolded before her, lit by the Luna Piena. Full Moon.

Cino embraced her from behind, pulling her close with his arms wrapped around her.

"You are like a beautiful dream in the moonlight," he whispered into her ear.

"Thank you for showing this to me. It is incredible, so perfect for tonight," she whispered back.

"I invited La Luna Piena just for you...the stars refused to come as they were jealous of your beauty tonight." Telling her in his slight, distinct Italian accent.

She smiled and turned to face him. Her beautiful face glowed from the moonlight shining through the huge windows. Cino cupped the back of her neck and head as he slid his fingers through her soft silky hair, pulling her lips to his. They shared a tender first kiss. He slowly caressed her as he ran his hands up and down her back. Victoria was overwhelmed by heated passion as she felt his awakened manhood and body press tightly against her. She pressed back against him while grabbing handfuls of black curls of his hair. Cino lifted her up into his arms and carried her to his bedroom, never once breaking their kiss, allowing it to sweep them away to a point they had both desired since their first meeting.

He laid her gently on the bed's 500 count, fresh, white Egyptian cotton sheets. He momentarily stood and admired her stunning, moon-lit profile sprawled on the bed as if in a Vargas pose.

Victoria rose from the edge of the bed on her knees while reaching up and slowly unbuttoning his shirt to reveal a thin swirl of black chest hair on his chiseled chest. Cino, in turn, took his kisses to her ear and neck as he stripped her of blouse, sliding both hands under her bra, stretching it so that it rose above her head and arms while still fastened. His full lips found their way to her warm, full breasts, charging them with intense electricity.

He was enthralled by the fill of her natural breasts. Victoria frantically tore at the top button of his pants as she unzipped them to free his powerful manhood; on fire and aching for her touch. Alternating between kisses and flicks of his hot, wet tongue, he slid down to her waist and beyond. His hands found their way beneath her lingerie and then he used his teeth and fingertips, gliding them down the path of her long beautiful legs until she was finally free of all clothing. Cino pulled her down on top of him. It was one of those rare occasions of two people meeting when their attraction literally takes their breath away. They both knew the universe meant for them to bond with soul fulfilling, savage sex, while feverishly descending into passionate lovemaking.

Chapter Fourteen

SUSPICIOUS MINDS

The Tripartite had become unnerved by the fodder being printed in the latest tabloids. So accurate was the recent gossip mentioned about two of their employers, they initially suspected each other of being a leak. A leak of confidentiality was the kiss of death in Hollywood. This was a town with more secrets than Langley, VA, CIA headquarters.

"'Loose lips sink ships,' yours and those around you," Irene volunteered to the other two.

Once they had dismissed themselves as the culprits, they went to work discussing who could have gathered their intimate, dead-on information. They had known each other long enough to trust each other completely as they had made a pact long ago that if one ever betrayed the others they would bring down all three. That's the way it had to be in order to enjoy unrestrained mutual trust amongst themselves.

The leak called for a strategy and awareness of everyone in their exposed circle, including the group of regulars at Schwab's. They even gave it a code name, "Operation Loose Lips." Their investigation commenced with the fielding of all the different people the three of them were exposed to during the day, from the gardeners, to the repairman, to potential phone taps.

These women were hardcore and serious when it came to their employer's privacy.

Not only were they upset that this kind of private information was reaching the tabloids and potentially compromising their employers, but the Tripartite were incensed over being cut out of the money making. They knew tabloids paid a fortune for verified information on the biggest stars.

"We're talking about maybe hundreds of thousands of dollars here, girls!"

"Now that really pisses me off!" chimed in Natasha. Not that they would have sold out their employers, who had also become dear and generous friends.

"I got a feeling it's close by," Maria-Angela said, as she frowned slightly and scanned the dining room of Schwab's with an expression of suspicion.

They planted false information in front of other employees while at work to see if they leak was coming from their workplaces. Only sharing the real stuff in a "sterile" location like Schwab's. Then they waited, and waited...for a month. Nothing showed up in the tabloids...except what was being discussed while at Schwab's. So focused on finding out who was profiting at their expense, they even clammed up at Schwab's at times, occasionally lowering their volume to a whisper between themselves.A change even Dotty noticed.

"Everything alright with you girls? You've been a bit low-key lately. Like in a serious state of mind."

"Oh, we're fine, dear, just dealing with some juicy gossip from work that is about to hit the papers. Of course, you know that we can't talk about it with you." Lilly makes the motion of zipping her lips.

"Top secret stuff!" adds Natasha, picking up on Irene's ploy.

Maria-Angela just stared with suspicion and a fake smile. She had not been too keen on Dotty lately, after guessing correctly about her secret affair with Sam.

"It's in the gut, I just don't like cheaters," she said to her friends coldly.

"I thought I'd plant that seed just to start flushing out the possibility of it being someone from here," Irene informed the Tripartite.

The women switched gears. This was serious and these three intended to get to the bottom of it. After all, their jobs were now potentially at risk. They were furious that someone was taking advantage of them collectively, and that was a bad move.

Maria-Angela was in quite the mood. She had been advised by her employer, screen legend, Ms. Vaught, "If one more of my private comments end up in the those dirty papers I'll be forced to clean house and start fresh with all of my employees."

"I am about to lose my job because of someone else making money off of my private conversations," fumed Maria-Angela.

"OK, I am going to say what we are all thinking. It could be Dotty. Hasn't anyone noticed how she always seems to be within earshot of our conversations? I think she is eavesdropping on all of the regulars here. Look how fast that story popped up about Victoria and that new hunk of Italian love of hers. Almost before she had a chance to taste those luscious lips of his. Hell, that's faster than even I can operate!" She glared in the direction of Dotty.

"I have a feeling quite a few of the famous regulars are starting to get suspicious of Dotty," Natasha added.

At that moment, two famous Rock Stars staggered in after jumping out of the back seat of a new silver Bentley and fighting off a few paparazzi flashing cameras in their faces. It was 8:00 a.m. in the morning and they were as sloshed as a drunk on payday.

"Table for two, Dearie," the female rock and roller quipped.

"Seat yourselves," Dotty softly yelled over her shoulder without looking.

"Are you kidding me, what kind of a dump is this joint?" the haggard 35-looking but 22 year old screamed. Before turning to her partner and climbing half way up his torso with one knee to get another taste of his tongue.

"Come on, baby, be nice. Ya gonna get us thrown out of this place too! And I'm starvin!" the rocker's equally famous escort pleaded.

"I don't give a shit. Why ya wanna eat here anyways? Just look at this dreary graveyard. I need music when I eat!" she slurred.

The Schwab's regulars had seen this scene played out a thousand times. The newbies along with a few tourists were horrified.

Dotty didn't blink an eyelash except to scribble down a few notes after realizing who it was.

The Tripartite were howling amongst themselves. Discreetly enough not to be rude, that is.

"What the fuck are you three bitches laughing at!" barked the female rocker.

That was enough to send both Irene and Maria-Angela to their feet.

"Ain't it obvious? We're laughing at the skanky heroin tramp that just walked in," launched Irene, moving fearlessly towards the famous music star.

"You talkin about me, bitch?" the barely comprehensible singer slurred back.

"We sure don't see any other nasty, cheap tramps standing around!" volleyed Maria-Angela as back up.

"That's it! Hit the bricks you two! We don't allow that kind of dirty talk and behavior in here." Dotty stepped in while calling out, "Sam, Jacques, we got a couple leaving, as in right now!"

"See what the fuck you've done! This is the second place we've been run outta and I'm fucking hungry! You are going home. And I'm going to get some food," the male Star told his companion right before she started sobbing and begging forgiveness from the women and everyone else in the place.

"Sorry, ladies." Dotty offered to Irene and Maria-Angela.

"No problem, I just hope it doesn't show up in MOUTH next week!" MOUTH was a leading Hollywood tabloid. Maria-Angela said it before she could check her anger.

Dotty tried to ignore it. But she suspected they were on to her.

Irene didn't say a word. She just rolled her eyes at Dotty. She was already charged up over the confrontation.

"Well, my dear friends, I guess the proverbial cat's out of the bag. I am quite sure she got the goddamn message this morning!" Natasha said in her angry Russian accent.

"Let's get the hell out of here before I lunge at Dotty!" Maria-Angela snapped, as Sam walked by.

"Something wrong, ladies? Sorry about those losers yelling at you," he offered.

"Thanks, Sam. Have a nice day." As the three pay and leave.

Chapter Fifteen

DISCOVERY

Jacques was always excited to see the infrequent but cherished super model, Chalon, when she graced their presence. He was especially fond of the big hug and kiss that she always bestowed upon him at their greeting.

"Ah, mon cherie! Finally you allow us to view your beautiful face in person again! We always miss you so much when you go away for long periods."

"Bonjour, mon amie! How is my favorite Frenchman in the whole world?" Chalon planted a kiss on each cheek. Just long enough for him to inhale her stunning beauty and steal a momentary essence of her soft cheek.

"Favorite Frenchman, uh? I want to be your favorite man!" he delivered with a huge smile, while swiftly swinging the door to Schwab's open for her entrance.

Chalon smiled and giggled as she cat-walked into the diner. As usual, she caused a stir upon her entrance, even among the jaded set. She was simply a walking, breathing creature of special beauty to behold. Tall, golden brown, with natural sandy blonde colored hair and ravishing green eyes. A look cooked up over hundreds of years of mixing in America. She was at the top of her game and currently the most sought after super model on the planet. She was also sweet, charming, and had not lost her small town San Fernando Valley roots. Making a point of being polite to everyone, regardless of their station in life.

The Tripartite was thrilled to see her, as they were always the first ones greeted with kisses for all, and were always instantly swept up in her glamour and beauty. But not today!

The three women had more pressing matters at hand. They had narrowed down their potential leak of their private conversations down to Schwab's. The other possibilities of anyone stealing their private gossip had failed to produce any results. That left Schwab's. But who at Schwab's was the question?

Chalon had just graced three of the top fashion magazines in the world this month and was streaking from New York to Paris to Tokyo for work. Now commanding $30,000, per day, she was the highest paid model in fashion.

Dotty wasted no time in fishing for details of the super model's personal life and the male stars whom she had left behind as road kill.

"I try to keep it quiet, Dotty, you know, like your life." Letting the comment roll off her tongue in a slightly defensive tone.

She had hoped to forget the last bad split, which resulted in a coke and sex binge. Chocking it up to youth.

"Oh, I understand. I just like to hear about your fabulous life. And what a life you must live! So exciting!" Gushing like a fan, Dotty hoped to reel some information in.

"No interviews today, just some fruit, bagel, and tea please." Chalon ended the exchange with a wave and a smile directed at Michael Deeves while excluding any further eye contact with Dotty.

She was experienced enough to know how to shut them down and place the wall up.

"My personal life will show up in the rags soon enough, no need in having to beat a dead horse to death," she thought and sighed to herself.

"Umm...had I forgotten how handsome that writer was? What was his name?" Her eyes twinkled towards Michael Deeves.

"I wonder if he's sold anything yet. There might be a part in it for me. A girl's always gotta have a plan B.

"There are yachts to by, villas to staff, and careers to conquer. Plan while you're on top, never in desperation" was the advice an older, ruling diva of the jet-set, Ms. Mae Vaught, had once given at breakfast. Advice she'd taken seriously.

She intended to have a long, successful career. If only she could get her deadly attraction to handsome men, private jets, and two-day parties under control. At least she had walked away from the last one with a $25,000 bracelet to soothe her broken heart, even though it was she who had left him. He demanded too much control over her intercontinental travel.

"But, oh, did he make her sizzle!" A thought that always made her smile.

"So, so handsome, but dangerous. Just the way I like 'em."

"Dotty will get none of that out of me ever again. I don't trust someone who is always asking questions about your personal life." Bringing herself back to reality as Dotty delivered her breakfast.

Chapter Sixteen

DETECTIVE GOLDMAN

Detective Goldman would learn that one of the first to discover Dotty's dark side was Victoria Steele and Cino Salvaggio.

Two months into their love affair, Cino and Victoria showed up for breakfast at Schwab's. Both laughing and holding on tightly to each other as they entered the diner.

There was no mistaking that they had become an item, or the heated passion that existed between them. They couldn't keep their hands off of each other. The stroking of the cheek, the brushing of hair out of the eyes, slight innuendos that sent clear signals of a very intimate relationship.

They were quite striking to see together. The two garnered lingering stares wherever they went because of their combined handsomeness.

Cino and Victoria seemed oblivious to the world around them.

"Bonjour, Mademoiselle Steele e Monsieur!" Jacques greeted the two upon arrival at Schwab's

"E Madame, can't you see!" Cino interjected with a big smile and a wink towards Jacques in jest.

"Mai oui! Of course!" he replied smiling while thinking, "You lucky SOB!"

The two made their way to their usual spot at the counter, trying their best to be as inconspicuous as possible.

"Morning, you two love birds of paradise!" mumbled Dotty in a low, "it's just between us" kind of whisper. Pretending to participate in a confidential moment between the three of them.

"Hi, doll, how are you this gorgeous morning?" beamed Victoria. Oblivious to anything negative in the world around her.

"Buongiorno!" Cino greeted her.

Dotty poured coffee for them after serving them. Managing to keep herself within earshot just in case there was something important to pick up on.

"Are you ready for a sexy treat this morning, amore?" Cino asked her with his mouth breathing near her ear.

Normally, she did not go for PDA (public displays of affection), but with Cino it was different. She almost encouraged him while savoring every moment of it as the center of his universe.

"What is it?" she asked.

"Remember our little sexy photo session?"

She blushed and giggled like a college girl. "Of course, you naughty man."

"Well...Viola!" He declared, handing over an envelope to her delicate, manicured hands.

It contained photos inside. They snuggled, laughed, and kissed while going through the set of private pictures. Victoria could barely contain herself from screaming with delight as she glanced through them.

"Hmmm, I look quite good, don't you think?" she asked

"Good enough to have for breakfast...right here, right now! How about I lay you on the counter and we give everyone a show!" he answered.

The pictures left behind of Victoria were a bit risqué, but certainly not X-rated. It had all been done in the heat of fun and passion. She glanced at the last one showing her in a beautiful black spider, breast tipped negligee. One she'd bought especially for him as it matched the one Sophia Loren had worn in Love Italian Style.

"That's my favorite one! Sophia now has competition!" he proudly proclaimed as he leaned over to kiss the back of her neck.

Victoria quickly gathered up the photos and placed them in the envelope and slipped it under her plate as if to hide it while engrossed in Cino's embrace, to prevent the hovering Dotty from catching a glimpse.

"I am truly having the time of my life with the wonderful man," she thought.

"I can't ever remember being this totally happy and in love. So far, he's proven to be sincere, devoted, independent, and intelligent. Not to mention being the sexiest male creature I've ever laid eyes on." She secretly hoped Hollywood wouldn't ruin him like it has so many others.

"Oh no! I'm late...very late! Finance meeting this morning. No money equals no pictures, and no studio!" she said while hurrying to leave.

"You go, amore, I'll take care of this and call you later," Cino said to Victoria as he delivered a quick kiss to her.

"I'll fix dinner tonight in front of the fire." As she gathers her things.

"Va bene," he replied.

Victoria rushed out the door and on to the studio.

Cino finished, paid Dotty, and raced out the door ten minutes later. Running late himself.

Dotty did a fast sweep of the counter and looked down at an envelope that hit the floor. As it hit the floor, she saw photos fall out. They sent her heart racing.

"Oh God!" she managed in a quiet tone to herself while trying to contain her rush of excitement and panic.

Dotty instantly recognized Victoria and Cino in them, swiftly gathered them up and into her apron pocket for safekeeping before Sam or the others could see them. Her heart pounding and her devious mind already at work on how to exploit them for a payoff.

Cino and Victoria were unaware of the forgotten pictures. Each assuming the other had them in their possession. They were focused on their new love for each other, and both were in a hurry that morning.

"These pictures are too hot to sell to the tabloids. I have to figure out how to leverage them without stepping over that line of blackmail. This could be my golden opportunity to move on. One I've been dreaming of for years!" Her compass of rationality had long ago careened out of control. Dotty never once demonstrated a thread of ethical character beneath her facade of trustworthiness. Unless, of course, it was to defend her own deceitful actions. Perhaps it was the universe's justification for her plain, homely looks and unrelenting greed. It was all the more odd seeing how the parents that raised her were two of the kindest, most ethical people on the face of the earth. Even Dotty's sweet, fake facade was beginning to lose its shine and effectiveness. The dark side does that to people. She often found herself driven by an innate feeling of detachment when using material that had the potential to ruin a person's life. It was as if she was born with pictures in her DNA.

"Should I do this on my own? Can I? I need to think on this for a few days."

"My daughter will be grateful one day. She will understand that I did all of this for her." Toying with an excuse to make herself feel better.

Make no mistake, it was for Dotty when Dotty did despicable things to others.

Chapter Seventeen

DOTTY'S PROPOSITION

Working out her newest plan in her head, Dotty was deep in thought.

"I can do this myself. If I do this right, I could make enough dough to walk away from the tabloids. I've had enough of the creeping around like a good little waitress, always snooping and graveling for little morsels of secret info to sell. At least I've been discreet and have never been found out about my little side job. I don't think I could live with myself if my daughter found out. Hopefully, she would understand it was all for her.

Once again trying to justify her dirty dealing.

Dotty approached screen writer Michael Deeves with the intention of striking a deal that would benefit both of them.

"Good morning! How's my number one screenwriter?"

"Great! How's my number one waitress?"

Silently reminding herself, "God … how I loathe that big loser sign that hangs around my neck all day, "Dotty, the sweet, homely, loser WAITRESS!"

"I'm feeling particularly fabulous today! Because I have some great news for you!"

"Me?" What could Dotty possible have to offer me? he wondered. Swiftly searching his brain for any kind of possible professional or personal connection to Dotty outside of Schwab's.

"Yes, you! What if I told you to bring your best script to me and I could guarantee it would go directly into the hands of the head of a major studio? How's that for good news!" She smiled at Deeves.

"Whoa! You're kidding right? Oh man! That would pretty much scorch my britches!" he said, not knowing if this was for real or not.

"Well, I've got a fire extinguisher right over there. Let me know if I need to get it after I tell you that I am serious and can deliver. Let's talk business!" Dotty's replies, ready to deal. She knew Michael had talent.

"You got it! I am all ears, Dotty!" Deeves said.

Dotty shook hands with Deeves and struck a deal that would allow her to share in the profits from his percentage of worldwide gross profit.

Michael would bring his best screenplay to the table, the one great writers always saved for the big break.

Dotty was right about Michael Deeves. After reading the script that night, it did not disappoint.

She now had the merchandise in hand and was ready to move on to phase two. The delicate, yet persuasive, sell to Ms. Victoria Steele. She was confident that her little cache of personal photographs would sway Ms. Steele to make up her mind in favor of Dotty's deal.

Chapter Eighteen

BLACKMAIL

"Hello, Victoria! May I have a word with you alone before you leave this morning?"

The risk Dotty was about to embark upon was the greatest in her life. Something in her DNA pushed her to take the leap.

"Of course, Dotty, are you alright? You seem nervous or distracted." Victoria shared her feelings of sincere concern. She had known Dotty for over six years.

"Well, I don't know quite how to approach this as it is an unusual situation. So, I'll just present it to you. I know you are hugely successful at what you do, Ms. Steele, therefore I would like to present to you an opportunity to kill two birds with one stone."

"Just what do you mean? I am a bit confused here." She searched her mind in an attempt to figure out it out. "What opportunity could Dotty possibly have to offer me professionally?" Victoria's professional force field was instantly activated. Her previous concern for Dotty's well-being had now morphed into guarded caution.

"You see, our resident Schwab's writer, the very talented Michael Deeves, has given me his best script in the hopes that you would review it. I know you have the ability to green light projects with the snap of your fingers and I was hoping to return some photographs of yours after the launch of the project." She exhaled as if she was almost ready to faint. Praying to herself that she had gotten her veiled message across.

"What on earth are you talking about? What photos are you referring to that makes you think I would get involved in what sounds like some kind of blackmail scheme," Victoria stated with Arctic coldness.

"The ones that are clearly of a personal nature between you and your new lover, the Italian. I believe they were accidentally left here one morning," Dotty states with a wicked look in her eyes.

"I see, so you and this writer want to strong arm me into a picture deal for this writer. Is that it?" she asks.

"They are so personal; I just want to see that they are back in your hands. And perhaps you could do a favor for me in return." Attempting to steer clear of outright blackmail.

"Like a multi-million-dollar movie deal?"

"Gosh, that sounds like an awful lot of money."

"Get off it, Dotty, your little smarmy, innocent waitress days have just been flushed down the toilet. Give me the fucking script. Just when are you planning on returning the pictures?"

"As soon as the contracts are signed, and I secure seal my share of the movie's profit as producer. I'm sure you will thank me later. It is a fantastic script!"

"What the hell would a low-life, greasy waitress like you know about producing a movie? Here's how this is going to go down, so listen carefully. I will read your scammy cohort's script, and IF I like it I will proceed. IF I do not like it, you are going to return my goddamn pictures or I will go to the police regardless of the public damage. You … dear sweet Dotty had better hope and pray that I like this script or you might be serving up 15 to 20 years instead of eggs and bacon. I will do all that I can to make sure your life is toast. How's that for your new menu? You'll have my answer in two days." Furious, Victoria stormed out of the diner.

Victoria rushed home to check the purse she had carried that morning as she was sure Cino had given her the photos. Hoping that perhaps only one had slipped out of the envelope and Dotty was bluffing.

"Did I give them back to Cino? I can't remember." Frantically calling Cino to verify.

"Hi, love, did I give you our photos we looked at together while at Schwab's the other day? Please tell me I did?" Trying not to sound too panicked.

"No, my love. I thought you took them with you. I don't have them. What is wrong?" he asked in a protective manner.

"I can't seem to find them. Don't worry though, I will look around some more, I am sure they are at the house somewhere." She didn't dare tell him that she had just been blackmailed by Dotty, the waitress at Schwab's, who was now angling for a movie deal!

"Let me know. I don't want those photos of you in any stranger's hands." Showing no concern for himself.

"OK, I will see you later tonight." Victoria tried not to sound upset.

"Ciao amore," Cino signed off.

* * *

Dotty was beaming with her self-perceived cleverness as she contemplated her not as yet completed successful business deal.

"Haha! They can call me Dotty the waitress if they want to, but they'll soon find out who the smart business woman is!" Bragging to herself.

"I've learned a lot from slinging the grease in this joint all these years." Speaking aloud to herself as she stared straight ahead, with glazed over eyes, while wiping the same spot on the counter in a circular pattern over and over again.

She wasted no time in sharing the good news with Michael Deeves.

"Michael, the deal is done! We'll know if we have a confirmed green light in two days!"

"What! Are you joking, Dotty? I can't believe it! WOW! Thank you from the bottom of my heart. And thank you for believing in my work." He was stunned by the immense kindness of this woman and sat for a minute in a semi state of shock.

"Who would've figured little ol' Dotty as a big movie deal mover and shaker! If this movie is a hit, she deserves every nickel she gets and then some," he thought as he smiled to himself in disbelief.

Michael was completely oblivious to the shady scheme that Dotty had, unbeknownst to him, used in swinging a potential movie deal for getting his work presented to the head of American International Films. He would later find out that he was duped along with almost everyone else who thought they knew "kind, sweet Dotty."

One week later, Michael was sitting in the huge plush office of Victoria Steele, CEO of American International Films.

"Michael, your project is quite good. Tell me, why go through Dotty?" Victoria inquired.

"She suggested that you might like it, and in this town and business, a guy has to use every angle or opportunity," he volunteered.

"So, you two worked on this together?"

"Sorta. Dotty worked on the "networking angle." If you know what I mean. I know it was bold to approach you and I hope you don't think it was too intrusive. I was just glad she offered this chance to me. I feel a bit intimidated talking to you about it. I normally submit through my agent. However, Dotty assured me that this was a win-win deal for all of us. Kinda funny don't ya think? Schwab's waitress brokers major movie deal!" Michael says with half a smirk on his face.

Deeves was innocent and unaware of the dirty, secret, back-hand dealing Dotty had used to broker the deal, as was Victoria to Michael's innocence.

"Just for the record … I most likely would have optioned it had it come through normal channels. For what it's worth, Michael, always remember this town has a long memory," Victoria delivered with her own cool smirk as she got up to leave the table without shaking his hand.

He was completely baffled by her last comments.

Victoria intended to use the situation with Dotty to her advantage. The script was good … . Damn good, she thought. She was certain she could work it into a successful film for millions in profit.

"But, I'll be damn if I let those two profit from it! I'll slice Dotty and her accomplice's legs off at the knee caps in due time." Victoria Steele was not a woman to be trifled with, especially by a conniving waitress who had taken advantage of a light, informal acquaintance. She intended for Dotty to learn a lesson. A lesson taught with hard jail time for blackmail and extortion.

Chapter Nineteen

INVESTIGATION CONTINUED

"So, Sam, let's go over this one more time," Rocco said during his interrogation of O'Brien.

"Dotty had started coming in twenty to thirty minutes early about two months ago. She knew Jacques and I would be on time so she didn't seem to be too worried about being here alone for a short time," Sam said.

"Why did she start coming in early?" asked Detective Goldman.

"We kinda had a falling out," answered Sam.

"Why was that?"

"Dotty and I had been kinda friendly."

"So, you were sleeping together?" Rocco asked.

"Yes, and I ended it because of my girlfriend. I didn't like the way Dotty behaved around me," he told Rocco.

"And Dotty didn't like that you ended it?"

"No."

"Was there a fight between the two of you?"

"What do you mean by 'a fight'? If you are trying to say I would harm her, you're crazy!"

"Calm down, Sam. I'm just trying to gather the facts, no matter where they lead. Did her husband find out?"

"No, not that I know of. She never mentioned it to me."

"OK, if you think of anything else you wanna tell me, let me know, Sam. I intend to find whoever did this. Dotty was one of our own, the Schwab's family."

Rocco left Schwab's with more questions than when he had arrived.

Sam thought about the questioning and talked to Vivien about it. They both thought it best for them to speak directly to Detective Goldman. After all, the fight between her and Vivien had been overheard by Jacques. Not mentioning it might appear suspicious, and they had nothing to hide. Or so it appeared.

* * *

"Jacques do you have any idea why anyone would harm Dotty? Have you seen anything out of the ordinary since you have been here pretty much the same time, everyday, as Dotty?" Rocco asks Jacques, who was pretty shaken up.

"Well, I just can't imagine anyone doing this to Dotty. I don't know if this is important, but I did witness a pretty nasty fight between Sam, his new girlfriend Vivien, and Dotty a while ago."

"How nasty?"

"Nasty enough that Vivien threatened Dotty over Sam. I mean physically!" Jacques said, hoping it would be of some use.

Jacques was unaware that Sam had already told Rocco about the fight. Sam's version anyway.

"Did you know that Sam and Dotty were carrying on an affair? It was none of my business of course, but I think several people knew," Jacques continued.

"So, you are saying Vivien was jealous and got angry?"

"No no no. It was the other way around. From what I overheard—I was in the main dining room and they were arguing in the kitchen—Dotty was the one who had become jealous. Sam had ended it with her. I think Vivien showed up by accident that morning to give Sam his wallet."

"How serious was the fight?"

I heard Vivien tell Dotty that she would kill her if she didn't stay away from Sam."

"You actually heard her say kill?"

"Well, something to that effect. It may not have been that exact word. But she made it clear that she would get violent with Dotty. I mean, she purposefully stepped on her toe as she walked out."

"Stepping on someone's toe is a helluva lot different than killing them, Jacques," clarified Rocco.

"Maybe she didn't mean kill, you know my English gets messed up sometimes."

"Who was the first to find Dotty the morning of the murder?"

"Sam and I arrived at the same time. Normally, we'd meet up with Dotty in the kitchen for a cup of coffee together. She started coming in early after the fight. I think they were trying to avoid being alone together."

Rocco thought it interesting that Jacques hadn't revealed his involvement in the blackmail deal Dotty had cooked up with the pictures of Miss Steele and Mr. Salvaggio. The details of this were reviewed from Dotty's email account. Thanks to Elsa.

He'd save that hammer for another day. First, he wanted to see where the investigation of his primary suspects led.

"Had you ever had any disagreements with Dotty, Jacques?"

"Moi! Mon dieu! We worked well together for many years!" Lying about his angry resentment after Dotty had cut him out of the Victoria Steele scam, at the last minute. At the time, he saw the deal as his opportunity to take his payoff and make his way back to France to buy a small winery. Dotty double crossed him and cut him out of the deal altogether and moved on to Michael Deeves, her unsuspecting pawn.

Michael had been a sure bet, whereas Jacques carried with him too many negatives and a criminal edge, Dotty had decided. How one cleans up blackmail to make it acceptable was something only the ruthless mind of Dotty Henderson could equate.

Chapter Twenty

THE TRUTH COMES OUT

After being yelled at by the boss of one of the more notorious tabloids, "Yes, sir!" The less than enthused, dejected reporter replied. Not yet realizing that that story could make or break his career. He was just young enough to still believe in the old, grand, ethical ideas of journalism.

"You get a crack team together and dig up everything that woman has ever sold us! And then you make sure you have a team shadowing every move of her husband, ex-boyfriend, aunt, uncle, or shoeshine boy! Now hit the bricks!" the overweight, cigar chomping editor barked.

Not to be outdone; Psst magazine simply splashed "Naughty Dotty Gets Knifed: live with a swagger, die by the dagger!"

"Long time Schwab's waitress swished and fished around the famous hangout for dirt on it's famous clientele. So, for all you famous folks out there that used to frequent good ol' Schwab's, be on notice that your waitress has been whipping up more than just your breakfast. How about a nice fresh dish of Movie Star DIRT! Fresh off the press!"

The National Radar, one of Dotty's former cash cow tabloids, was the first to link Dotty's murder to the stars. It blew the lid off of her undercover side job as a snoop who stole information from her famous customers. It was merciless in its blaring, train horn-like headline, "Snuffed out waitress was a ruthless snitch on the Stars!" Subparagraph with, "Was this a revenge murder?" So much for protecting your former sources.

MOUTH, another weekly rag, headlined like a five alarm fire: "Schwab's' Secret Snoop sells her last Scoop!"

"Twisted, Trusted waitress snitched on famous customers to the tabloids for millions over the years!"

Both tabloids followed with a recent list of major scoops that had been provided by Dotty. Each published a special daily edition running a different article sold to them by Dotty everyday.

Circulation soared!

The revelation of Dotty as a primary source smashed the murder investigation wide open. It was now clear that Rocco and Elsa were going to be handling a rare and unusual case even for Hollywood, and its citizens suddenly became quite nervous.

"But, sir, we are stirring a witch's brew with this story. People's lives will be damaged," pleaded a reporter to her boss.

"Yeah, a few careers will be damaged...including yours if you don't get the hell out of here and get this story out on time...on a daily basis! This is the newspaper business, my dear girl. It's about circulation and that equals money! Got that! This is a golden egg that has befallen us. Now scram!" the hard driving editor let loose.

The world wide web was set aflame with each new famous name published on a daily basis. It was as if it were a fresh log thrown on a burning fire for fuel.

Coverage further exploded when the number of abortions had by music superstar Venice Adriatica was revealed, causing her to have a public meltdown, culminating with the shaving of her head in the middle of a performance along with public disorientation.

This frothed into a downward spiral of Hollywood. Little did the world know, they hadn't seen "nuttin" yet!

Movie proposals were flying between Hollywood studios like a time/space-bending flying saucer. Warp speed was considered too slow to capture the frenzy of this story on film.

All the nut jobs and fame whores in Hollywood came of the woodwork claiming responsibility for the murder and demanding an "exclusive" televised confession. Paid of course.

The hot, steamy, personal photos of American International Film CEO, Victoria Steele, and her Italian lover, Cino Salvaggio, were discovered in Dotty's safety deposit box, along with a copy of the film contract between her, Michael Deeves, and American International Films. Rocco would handle interviewing Ms. Steele and Cino while Elsa moved in on Michael Deeves.

Meanwhile, the Tripartite were singing like canaries, 80% of which was their version of the hypothetical, mixed with a high dose of revenge.

"I was the first to suspect her devious behavior. I just sensed it," Maria-Angela proudly told Rocco.

"Dotty all of a sudden became extra attentive towards us after we realized parts of our personal conversations amongst ourselves started showing up in those horrible rags. We knew for sure it wasn't one of us sharing information," Irene joined in with a tone of utter disdain.

"We set a trap for her. We made a few things up and waited to see if she took the bait," Natasha quickly added.

"Yep, and whatcha know! Low and behold, there it was! In the rags the following week!" interjected Irene.

"That's when we knew. It was Dotty." Natasha ending Irene's sentence like a twin sister.

"We were planning on confronting her, but thought we should tell Sam first. Then we discovered they were hanging out between the sheets together! I was the one to figure that out! I mean, GOOD GOD! This woman was VERY busy!" Maria-Angela said while throwing her arms up in the air in a gesture of unbelievability.

"We couldn't make this up, it's that unreal," Irene stated in a lowered voice with a sense of incredulity.

"I guess everyone in showbiz is nervous about their employees' ears and mouths after that snake Dotty," Maria-Angela said.

"Can you blame them!! That witch has given us all bad names. If she wasn't dead, I'd kill her myself!" she continued.

"My employer is afraid to say anything around me except for good morning, and that comes with a side glance of suspicion. This, after eight goddamn years!" fumed Irene.

"Wow, so you at least get a hello! I get a 'Hmmm?'" Natasha answered.

"I have to admit, girls, I'm anticipating every new revelation, I just can't help it! Is that so bad?" Irene admitted.

"Girl, you know we all do!" said Natasha. They laughed in chorus.

In this day of instant global communications, nothing and no one was safe. Gone were the days of privacy outside of glamour events.

The constant hunger of the voyeur driven, reality TV, overweight couch potato elite was what drove it all.

The public demanded intrusion into the lives of the famous and the rags paid handsomely for it. Dotty tapped into the reporting of the private lives of the famous. Her murder was a visual feast for the tabloid piglets fighting for a turn at the teat of sleazy details about her. The more the public read the bigger their appetite grew. Not even the best scriptwriters in Hollywood could have outdone this unfolding drama.

Chapter Twenty-One

FOLLOW UP CINO/VIC

Cino and Victoria phoned Rocco prior to him contacting them.

"She was blackmailing us with personal photos that I had accidentally left after a breakfast with Cino." Victoria started off.

"Why didn't you notify the police?"

"And risk it going public? You and I both know that the integrity of the police, when it comes to celebrities, is as porous as a tea strainer," she said dryly to Rocco.

"So, you were very angry with her, knowing that she could damage your career?" Rocco proposed.

"I was beyond upset. I was furious, and wanted to wring her neck. But I was not motivated to murder someone over a few risque photos. They were not X-rated, but they could have definitely negatively impacted my career as head of a major motion picture studio," she stated honestly.

"So you gave in?" asked the detective.

"Instead of returning the photos, she used them, along with Michael Deeves, as a shake down to force a movie deal from me in lieu of selling the pictures to a tabloid," she continued.

Cino sat quietly while clearly trying to contain his fury as Victoria gave their explanation.

"The film is in production. I told Mr. Deeves that I would have optioned it had it come to me through legit channels. He seemed a bit surprised by that. I proceeded with the project because I made a business decision that I believed would be in the best interest of the studio as a money making venture," she informed him.

"And you didn't mind being strong armed?" the detective asked.

"What kind of stupid question is that, Mr. Detective? Of course we did! We are still outraged!" Cino interrupted.

"Excuse me, sir! If I need any information from you I will ask you directly." Rocco managed to contain his flash of anger.

"We were going to present everything to the police at a time when we thought it would have the least amount of risk," Victoria further explained.

>$<

Michael Deeves told private detective Elsa Wagoner the truth when interviewed.

"I know Victoria Steele, the head of American International Films, very well. Well enough that she would accept a script from me knowing that she has the power to green light a film to be made. And she would not mind at all if I presented this to her. Those were her exact words to me, Ms. Wagoner," he stated.

"Did you ever speak to Ms. Steele directly regarding the project? And was Dotty present?" inquired Elsa.

"Yes, and no. I did meet with Ms. Steele regarding the project, and no, Dotty did not attend. I will tell you this, the meeting felt a bit strange towards the end."

"What do you mean?" Elsa asked.

"I mentioned to her how odd it was to be sitting there with her via Dotty. That I was blown away to have this opportunity presented to me through Dotty, who I've known for a long time. I just never expected her to pull something like this out of a waitress pocket," he said while appearing perplexed.

"I assumed Dotty was just trying to help me out as a friend, and profit from it of course, which is to be expected if she was to act as a go between," he continued.

"You didn't think it odd that the head of a major film studio would trust the judgment of a waitress over that of professional writers' agents for million dollar film projects?" Elsa pushed for more information on his involvement.

"Not in this town or business. Dotty had access to a lot of different people at Schwab's. You know for yourself what the clientele is like there," Michael said with a tone of incredulity.

"And the studio liked the project?" asked Elsa.

"Not only did they like it, Ms. Steele told me personally that had it come to her through normal channels she would have jumped on it," he said proudly.

It began to appear that even clever Michael Deeves had been expertly manipulated. There was no doubt, Dotty was a pro.

Michael was dumbfounded to learn that he had been unknowingly used like a pawn.

But had he? Had he allowed himself to be played by Dotty, fully aware of his benefit regardless of how she got the deal done? He'd thought he was far too observant for the tricks of this town to get past him.

"It was refreshing, in a way," he thought.

He was somewhat pleased to discover that he hadn't become completely jaded to it all at this young age. Yet, as a writer, there was still plenty for him to learn in life. Suddenly realizing that his mere innocent involvement in this murder was a once in a lifetime opportunity for a writer.

"I've been given a front row seat to potentially one of the greatest Hollywood dramas in decades." Thinking to himself as he pulled out his beat up old laptop and notepad and went to work.

"There may be other writers in this town working this story, but none of them have the kind of the inside seat like I do." He smiled to himself.

He called Elsa and Detective Goldman to offer his help.

"I know these people inside out, better than anyone. I've sat watching them for the last six years. That's my job as a writer. To observe." Extending his expertise to what almost sounded like a plea.

"I know, Michael. Remember, I've known you for five of those six years. Besides, we haven't exactly cleared you up of your involvement."

"At least let me be a source of information. Like with that stranger that started coming around and acting weird around Dotty a few weeks ago. I think he was after her fingerprints or DNA. I know how that works. For Christ's sake, I researched and wrote about it!" Attempting to make his point of reliability.

"What guy? And exactly when did this happen?" Rocco decided then and there that maybe Michael could add something to the investigation.

"Alright, but understand I cannot let you in on anything about how the investigation is proceeding." The hesitant detective relented.

"One more thing, I'm pretty sure I saw this guy snapping a picture of Dotty with his cell phone. He thought he was being discreet, but I picked up on it. I saw him point it in her direction several times and you could hear the clicking sound. He didn't have the sound turned off. Dotty must have heard him as well because she suddenly turned to face him when it clicked and he quickly put it away. I tell you, this man knows something. I think you need to find him." Michael was pleased with the assistance he'd just given.

Michael was no different that the rest of the city in snapping up every word being printed in the daily special editions of the tabloids, newspapers, and industry trades. He began to compare notes with what he read and what he remembered from his front row seat at Schwab's.

"Oh, she was good. She was damn good. Had everybody who knew her fooled, including me!" he ran over and over in his head.

"Not everything is meshing as I remember it though. The way Dotty came to me out of the blue with carte blanche access to Victoria. Something is wrong with that whole picture," he kept thinking to himself.

"My god, we must all look like potential murderers with motives. She'd worked us all over in one way or another." Suspicious, yet perplexed at the same time.

"I need to speak to Victoria. If something is wrong because of Dotty, I need to make this right."

Chapter Twenty-Two

WOODWORK

Michael was no different than the rest of the city in snapping up every word being printed in the daily special editions of the tabloids, newspapers, and industry trades. He began to compare notes with what he read and what he remembered from his front row seat at Schwab's.

"Oh, she was good. She was damn good. Had everybody who knew her fooled, including me!" he ran over and over in his head.

"Not everything is meshing as I remember it though. The way Dotty came to me out of the blue with carte blanche access to Victoria. Something was wrong with that whole picture," he kept thinking to himself.

"My god, we must all look like potential murderers with motives. She'd worked us all over in one way or another." He was suspicious yet perplexed at the same time.

"I need to speak to Victoria. If something is wrong because of Dotty, I need to make this right."

He rang Victoria's office immediately. He had to clear his suspicions about Dotty's involvement with the movie deal.

"Good morning, American International Films, may I help you?" The receptionist picked up on the first ring.

"Would you please let Miss Steele know that Michael Deeves in on the line and that it is urgent that I speak with her? She will know who I am. She is producing one of my screen plays," he sputtered out nervously.

"Hold the line, sir."

He used to get a thrill out of being able to call "Victoria Steele" directly and expect a quick response as a result of his movie being made. Now it was with gremlins growling in his stomach.

He wasn't sure exactly how Dotty had presented this deal or how she truly finagled it. He only knew that his gut was telling him "something wasn't right."

"Hello, Michael … how can I help you?" Victoria was curt and strictly business.

"Ms. Steele, I wanted to speak to you about Dotty's involvement in this movie deal."

"You mean Dotty's and your involvement? I'm not sure I should be discussing this with you without the police involved."

"If you would be more comfortable with them present, I don't object to that at all, I just wanted you to know that I only recently figured out that I was mislead by Dotty as well."

"Go on. I'm listening."

"I really don't know how she swung this deal with you, but I wanted you to know exactly how I was brought into it. Dotty had simply approached me one morning, since, as you know from seeing me there, I was a regular at Schwab's. Anyway, she approached me one morning in a excited mood and asked 'how would you like to have your best project green lighted for a movie deal?' I thought she was joking at first, but she assured me she was dead serious. She told me she could take my project directly to you and have it reviewed. I didn't ask too many questions. I only assumed that because you were a regular of hers at Schwab's, there was perhaps some kind of friendship that allowed her to offer this to you." He exhaled with nervousness.

"There used to be, until she took advantage of it. Please continue."

"Well, I gave her the project that I felt was my best work. She said she wanted to work out a deal as the middle person if the project went forward. She seemed pretty certain that she could get you to green light it."

"I'm sure she did!" Victoria interjected.

"Long story short, I agreed to work out an agreement with her. I had nothing to lose if in fact she was that certain of her connection to you. Next thing I know, boom! I was getting a call from you about proceeding with the project! Needless to say I was ecstatic and incredibly thankful to her!"

"And you knew nothing else about the deal?"

"That's it. I was just thankful that you liked the project and gave me this huge opportunity."

"Michael, if this is as you say, I thank you for calling me and clarifying your involvement with Dotty. As we all now know, Dotty was anything but the innocent, kind person we thought she was. I can only tell you that there was much more going on than just a submission to me from a friend. You will no doubt learn of it through the investigation."

"I want you to know, Ms. Steele, up front, if there was anything underhanded involved with Dotty, I swear to you that I knew nothing about it and was as much of a pawn as anyone."

"Thank you for approaching me with this conversation, Michael. It sheds a lot of light on many things. I like you, and I like your project. I've told you before, it's good and we will make a lot of money on it. Feel free to stay in touch with me."

"You mean you are going forward with the project?" Breathing heavy.

"Yes."

"You will never regret it, Victoria … that I promise. Thank you for believing in me. I won't ever forget it." Michael cupped his face in his hands and was on the verge of tears. Tears of joy and relief. He was innocent and thrilled with life and this wonderful moment.

Chapter Twenty-Three

FAMILY

Ralph was stunned and numb, to say the least, to discover the secret life, bank accounts, and safe deposit boxes of his wife. His girlfriend wasn't. She had already hacked Dotty's email account, which was filled with salacious exchanges between her and Sam about their sexual romps. They also included notes on her prosperous endeavors with the tabloids.

Before she could download or copy most of the material though, Elsa, with legal authorization from the Los Angeles District Attorney's office, through Detective Goldman, locked and encrypted the account.

The slightly more than two million dollars in Dotty's accounts was motive enough to keep Ralph as a "person of interest" high on the list.

Moreover, his newly identified girlfriend, Celia Hammond, had been discovered by the IT forensic investigator after her email hacking and promptly added to the suspects list.

Ralph was confused, disturbed, and shocked at each new revelation about his wife.

"Who was this person I was married to all these years? I wonder if she found out about Celia?" Silently asking himself.

He felt the pain of loss with an extra helping of guilt for cheating on Dotty.

"I didn't start this. It was she who pursued me," he tried to convince himself.

"What the hell do I need with a young college girl!"

"If only she hadn't been so damn sweet, smart, and fucking sexy as hell with that hot little body. God the sex with that hot, wild creature was hot. How do I admit any of this without looking like the bad guy? What if Brit finds out? She'll never speak to me again." Now worrying about his and Dotty's daughter Brit.

"My daughter means the world to me. Maybe I should tell her first? Try to explain how it happened." Rolling over in his head a variety of paths to take.

Criminal Justice/Forensics UCLA senior Celia Hammond had met Ralph on a windy, rainy day while at a coffee shop. He said hello after she smiled at the nice looking older man.

She had always been attracted to older men as a young woman. Losing her father at 10 ten years old had a lot to do with it.

Celia had walked out to find a flat tire after leaving the coffee shop. Standing in the pouring rain while figuring out what to do, she was startled by the offer of assistance from the good looking man in the coffee shop.

"Hey there! What a bummer. Can I help you with that?" he offered.

"Oh, OK! I was just trying to figure out if I should ring AAA or try to do it myself." Knowing she didn't have the ability to change even a light bulb in this rain, let alone a tire.

"If you have a spare, I think I can help you with that. I'm pretty sure I can change that for you in no time." He kept asking himself why was he doing this? He loved his wife.

"That would be terrific. Only if you are sure it's no problem for you in this rain and all, and if you let me buy you a coffee afterwards." Slyly strategizing as to how she was going to get this sweet gentleman, who'd come to her rescue, into bed.

Ralph would later confide in a friend, "She's like a wild tiger in the sack. With a tongue that's as wicked as a circus whip in a lion's cage!" Bragging about his newly found sexual playmate.

"You lucky bastard! Does she have any horny friends?" his buddy asked, half joking and half hoping.

And so Ralph began his clandestine affair with the UCLA college senior.

Celia wanted to know all about Dotty after her death. She hacked into Dotty's email and bank accounts. That's when she discovered how much money she had been hiding from Ralph.

"So, she's screwing the boss. But, I wonder where all of that money came from. Definitely not from waitressing!" She contemplated the possibilities.

"I can't believe she carried on this whole other life without me knowing anything about it. I mean she was my wife dammit!" moaned Ralph to Rocco.

"That's usually the case, sir, I've seen it a hundred times," Rocco replied.

"But after 25 years, you'd think I'd have noticed something out of place."

"Did she know about your little secret?" Rocco dropped the unspoken "affair bomb."

"What are you talking about?" Ralph asked, looking surprised and nervous.

"We are talking about your hot little college girlfriend. Save the act, we know all about her and her slick computer skills. So, you knew about your wife's millions stashed away?" Elsa leaned over and asked.

"Yes, but only after Celia discovered it and told me about it. Along with the fact that my wife had been cheating on me with that son of a bitch boss of hers!"

"Explain to us what the plan was, Ralph. It's OK, we know more than you think. Was the plan "Knock off Dotty, collect the money, and live happily ever after your hot little young piece of ass? Was that it?" Elsa let him have it.

"To begin with, I only met Celia four months ago. She was the one who came after me. I had never cheated on my wife before. I loved Dotty," Ralph pleaded to the two investigators.

"I could have never, ever harmed my wife. Not for all the money in the world." Ralph broke down into tears. Sobbing uncontrollably.

"Sure, bud, they all say that. Until they are caught," Rocco tells Ralph.

"And save the teary eye act. This is Hollywood and you would never make it as an actor in this town," Elsa spewed out as a follow up to the "good cop, bad cop" routine.

"One thing is for sure, Mister, I'll nail Dotty's murderer. That you can take to the bank! I have a personal stake in this matter. That's all for now. And don't plan on leaving town with Miss Tiger Love. That's all for now. I'll be in touch," Rocco said sternly.

"I'll be around. Don't worry." Ralph said while appearing beaten down.

Rocco could tell the man was clearly in sincere mourning.

CHAPTER TWENTY-FOUR

STRANGER

A FEW WEEKS PRIOR TO DOTTY'S MURDER, THE WELL-DRESSED man in the tailored gray suit who had been hanging about the diner showed up at Dotty's home.

Her daughter, Brit, a 21-year-old student at UCLA, was studying at home when the doorbell chimed.

"Who is that? It's the middle of the day." Thinking, as she peered through the door's peephole.

"May I help you?" she asked

"Is Mrs. Dotty Henderson at home?" the distinguished gentleman asked.

"Who would like to know, and for what?"

"It's very important that I speak with her. If she's not home, could I find her at her place of employment, Schwab's?" he asked.

"How do you know where she works and what is this regarding? I'm her daughter and I handle all of her business affairs," Brit lied.

"Well then, may I speak to you, Miss? It is regarding a rather personal matter. I would be glad to speak to you out here if you are uncomfortable allowing me inside."

"No, its fine, my boyfriend is upstairs, and as you can see, you are on camera." He seemed professional enough she thought.

"Please, come in." She extended an invitation to the well dressed, gray-haired gentleman.

Brit directed him to take a seat in the living room as the composed man placed his expensive brown leather briefcase on his lap.

"Mark, I'll be right up after I speak to this gentleman about some business with mom!" She yelled towards the staircase as a back up to her pretense of not being home alone.

"Just what kind of personal matter is it, sir?" she asked the man.

"I'll get straight to the point. I am an attorney for a client searching for a potentially lost relative. We have substantial evidence that has led us to believe that this person may be your mother, Mrs. Dotty Henderson. There is one final step left to conclude the process: we will have to verify our search through DNA testing." Hoping that his explanation was short and to the point.

"Whoa! Who is this person you work for? We're not going to allow some stranger to just walk into our lives and turn over my mother's DNA. That's kind of crazy! That is also a gross invasion of privacy! Look mister, I really don't have time for this. Are you sure it is my mother you are looking for? Dotty Henderson? We are unaware of any lost relatives." Brit sounded defensive, yet curious.

"We are almost sure. We have been looking for a very long time. It's probably better that her daughter breaks the news to her anyway. Just in case the final step proves that she isn't who we are searching for. It would be a terrible thing for this to come from a stranger and end in disappointment. Does your mother have any information on her biological parents? It is not my intention to create any anxiety for Mrs. Henderson. I will add though, the outcome will determine the legal heir of a potential fortune in inheritance. I must stress once more that this can only be verified with DNA testing as a final step." He tried to make himself as clear as possible.

"Right. Who would do the testing? Where, and how? Why have we not heard anything regarding this before? No letter, nothing? You must acknowledge that this is surprising and very strange. What do you mean by information on her biological parents?"

"Your mother does know that she was adopted? The DNA sample can be accomplished by a simple test. I have one with me that I can leave for your mother." The stranger pulled an unopened DNA sample test kit from his briefcase. "We prefer to make contact in person with our clients when dealing with such delicate matters. As I indicated earlier, we have been conducting this search for a very long time. Only recently did our search point us in the direction of your mother. We do realize this can be quite a shock to people. We also realize that your mother may not have a complete understanding of her background. That is an emotional endeavor for anyone. We respect that." The man demonstrated a sense of delicacy while explaining to Brit as much as he could.

"This is a lot to take in out of the blue, sir," Brit replied, trying to hide her reaction to the jaw-dropping news that her mother had been adopted. If her mother knew, she had never told her about it.

"No one was sure that your mother even existed until an old document surfaced recently. Before that, we were unsure who we were searching for," he shared.

"How much of an inheritance are we talking about? And from who?" she asked.

"I'm afraid that I am not at liberty to answer either of those questions until we've concluded our last verification step of DNA testing. Thank you for your time, Ms. Henderson. I hope this has not been to unsettling for you. I will leave the kit for you along with my card and contact information. Please take some time to decide on how you and your mother would like to proceed." The stranger rose to excuse himself.

"Yes, thank you, I will. I'll have to think about this before addressing it to my mother and father. It would be awful to put them through this and it turned out to be a disappointment." Brit escorted the gentleman to the door.

Britt closed the door behind her, leaned backwards against it, and stared up at the ceiling in disbelief.

"That was weird and incredible. I don't know what to think? I wonder how much money he is talking about? Thousands maybe? But what kind of person can afford a private attorney to conduct a search for years? That sounds like they are very rich." Thinking to herself.

"But what if it turns out that mom is not the person? It would be devastating to put her and dad through this. It'd be like, believing you've won the lottery then being told that a mistake had been made. No … I'll wait, until I've gathered more information on my own. I need to speak with Aunt Marjorie before doing anything." Laying out a follow-up plan in her mind.

Brit Henderson had taken nothing in her physical appearance from her mother. She had been kissed with the good fortune of garnering the good-looking genes of her biological grandmother, and the handsomeness of her father Ralph. This lucky combination made for a stunning young beauty with female endowments to rival any starlet in town. Born with an independent nature and a high level of intelligence, she never needed much guidance from her mother. She had been spared the hard-edged view of the world her mother had gone through life with. An edge Dotty seemed to have been born with.

Make no mistake, this young woman carried with her cool, calculating manipulation skills. But hers had been polished with a different stone versus Dotty's. Brit's came from growing up as the beauty of the local school, thus placing her in an orbit where "how much money your family had" didn't matter. She was sought after by the boys, and later by young men, and, at times, by their fathers.

Squarely focused on her studies at UCLA, she had no doubt about her future and about eventually acquiring the tools needed for her to take what she wanted from the world. Whatever, and whoever, that may be. She didn't bat an eyelid when she intercepted the private representative of whoever it was inquiring about her mother.

Even at 21 years of age, Brit exuded an air of self-confidence that would have been admirable in most 35 year olds. It came naturally to her. A characteristic that unnerved people much older and experienced than she.

Later that evening, she had light heartedly asked her mother a few questions about her past.

"Mom, do you have any relatives you might have lost contact with that you can remember? And were any of them rich? And who was adopted?"

"No to the first question. Mom and Dad had no relatives except Aunt Marjorie that I know of. They lost most of their family before I was born in the Great Depression. They had it very tough you know," Dotty replied.

"Yes, I've heard that story from you a thousand times." Smiling to her mother.

"And no to the second question about unknown rich relatives. Trust me, dear, if they were rich, I wouldn't have lost contact with them!" They both shared a laugh over Dotty's answer.

"And If someone had been adopted, I would have known. So, no to your third question," she answered without hesitation.

Brit stored the information and worked over in her mind who this strange man might be, and what exactly was he after, beyond what was stated. She decided to start with a visit to her aged Aunt Marjorie.

* * *

Fallen, rustling leaves signaled the changing seasons. The morning air was crisp and breezy with bright sunshine. One could hear the crunch of dry, withered leaves underfoot as they walked down the street. The old lady's tiny cottage was on a cul de sac in the flats below the Los Feliz Hills. The street was quiet, except for the birds and crunching leaves. It was exactly as it must have looked in the 1940's. Not much had changed. All the little bungalows looked as they had when they were first built. The only discernible difference was the model of cars lining the quaint street. This was a rather comforting feeling considering an ever changing metropolis like Los Angeles.

"There it is, 1447 Crestwood. It looks like she might be home. I thought about calling ahead, but she rarely answered the phone these days," Brit thought.

"Shades are up, car parked in the driveway. I'll give it a shot. I wonder if she will remember me? Haven't seen her in awhile."

Brit lightly knocked on the door while still weighing in her mind how to approach the delicate subject of her mother's birth and past.

She heard faint footsteps stir inside, coming closer as they became slightly louder. A few minutes later she was startled to see a small set of little eyes framed by white hair peering through a sliver of pulled back white lace curtains, framing the glass panels on the side of the door.

"Yes?" a faint elderly voice spoke.

Brit was startled again when the voice appeared to come out of what seemed like the side of the wall. It was a small speakeasy, popular prior to intercoms back in the day.

"Hello, Aunt Marjorie, it's Brit, Dotty's daughter. I've come to visit. I hope you don't mind me popping in unannounced?"

"Dotty's daughter? Well of course, you come right in. I'll open the door. Just a minute dear" was the reply.

Brit heard the old lady fumble, switch, and unlatch what seemed like four locks and a deadbolt. The multiple clicking and clocking noise that emanated from inside came across as serious security.

As the old lady slowly pried the door open, she peeped around to look at Brit, then opened up with a big smile and open arms.

"Come in, dear, come in! What a pleasant surprise! My, my, my, you have grown up so beautifully. I don't know why, but it seems like yesterday that you were such a little thing," Aunt Marjorie told her. She hobbled on a cane to an overstuffed chair near the fireplace while swaying her right hand behind her in a motion for Brit to take a seat in a chair across from the fireplace.

"Can I offer you some tea or coffee, dear?"

"No ma'am. I was just thinking about you the other day and thought I should come by and give you a big hug. It's been so long since I've seen you."

"Isn't that nice. How is your mother, dear? She pops in on me every so often."

"She doing just fine. Aunt Marjorie, I wanted to ask you a few questions about mom's side of the family, and if there were any adoptions?"

The old woman's eyes and posture perked up and the inviting smile slowly faded into a look of suspense.

"What is it you want to know? Why the sudden interest?"

"I'm doing a project at my university on family histories and I'm trying to put ours together." Brit tried to be discreet about her intentions.

"Well, there isn't much to tell. Besides, us old folks just don't talk much about the past. Some things are better left behind."

"Was there something bad that happened?" She tried to pry something, anything out of her old aunt.

"I am getting older, Aunt, and I have a little interest in knowing more about my family history … curious, you might say." Brit disguised her answer as a weak plea.

"I see. Does your mother share your interest?"

"Not quite. In fact, she seems too busy to really give it any thought."

"You know your grandparents' people died during the War. And before that, we all suffered greatly during the Great Depression. It was a terrible thing." Her old aunt repeated the same line her mother had told her a thousand times.

"We all had a very difficult time. That darn War and all. Oh, for heaven's sake, I just don't like talking about it." Hoping the young girl would take a hint and leave well enough alone.

Aunt Marjorie had a habit of cocking her head to one side while glancing at you with one eyebrow arched high. It was a look full of dramatic slyness.

With her little shawl wrapped around her, she looked like Norman Rockwell's model for the ultimate grandma sitting by the fire.

Brit had a gut feeling Aunt Marjorie had been anything but a sweet ol' grandma.

"But, aren't there any photos of my grandparents, or their people?" Brit asked.

"Everything was lost in a fire years and years ago," the aunt replied.

"Well, auntie, thank you anyway. It's just that I get so sad when I think that I will have nothing to say about my family when my children come along." Displaying her poor little niece look.

"So, you said this information was just for you and your school? I do understand your curiosity. It's human nature," she said with a hint of sympathy.

"Of course, you know that I would treasure anything you would share with me." Brit begged.

"There is something I can tell you. But you know how much we like our privacy in this family. Just remember that." The aunt talked in a low voice.

"Well, I have some papers locked away that are to go to your mother or you after I pass. It has some information about your grandparents. You mustn't tell anyone about this. Not even your mother. These documents are to be seen only after my death. There are things in them that I swore never to divulge to anyone, ever."

"Is it something bad?"

"It depends on who's reading them. It could be good; it could be bad. I can't say any more than that."

"Jesus! It's like talking to the Riddler from Batman!" Brit thought to herself in frustration.

"How will we get them?"

"George has been given instructions in my will to provide them to you," the aunt answered.

George was the old lady's only son. Brit wasn't even sure of her old aunt's age, nineties she guessed, or how she was even related to them. In reality, she was a little afraid to even find out. Everything about her mother's family had always been so cryptic.

She was starting to entertain the idea that the gentleman who showed up at the house may actually be legit.

"Aunt Marjorie, you don't know what a burden you've taken off of my mind. I just feel so incomplete sometimes, not knowing anything about my grandparents other than where they were from, and where they are buried." Pretending to be relieved in front of her aunt.

Her aunt had just stirred up her curiosity even more. She was now convinced that there was something more to this. Far more than what was being said, by all involved.

"I am glad I was able to put your mind at ease, my little angel. Now, you remember, this is our little secret."

"Yes, Aunt Marjorie, my lips are sealed," she answered. While thinking, "But, my dear aunt, there is a lot that I intend to "unseal" as fast as I can." As she gave her old, frail aunt a gentle goodbye hug.

* * *

The next morning, Brit phoned the gentleman in the gray suit straight away.

"Good morning, sir. I've given our discussion some thought. In order for us to proceed with the request of your client, we will be asking a few questions.

"First, if it is possible, we would like to know the name of your client if we are to release something as personal as a DNA sample. Secondly, should my mother turn out to be the individual you are looking for, what kind of protections will she be entitled to? Thirdly, what is the amount of inheritance at issue? And finally, how did you become aware of my mother's adoption?" She was proud of her professional presentation.

"I'm afraid I may not be able to divulge to you the identity of my client because of privacy and security concerns. I will, however, share this request with them for further instructions. If your mother is the individual that we are searching for, her protection is laid out in a legal codicil that has been put into place, a complete step by step process in helping her along the way, along with the assistance of her newly found family, should she be the one, of course. I am unable to inform you of any dollar amount except to say it is quite large. Should I say more than that, it has the potential to put your mother and her entire family at risk should anyone outside of your family discover this. Finally, your mother's adoption was discovered during the course of our extensive investigation, involving many people, that has led us to your mother's doorstep. Suffice it to say we have spent decades and millions of dollars searching for a lost family member. At this point, the DNA test would hold all the answers for us, your mother, and her family," he concluded.

"Miss, hello, Miss? Are you still there?" There was a long pause of silence on the other end, long enough for the gentleman to wonder if Brit was still on the line.

"Yes … yes, I'm still here. Thank you for your time in discussing this. We will wait for your response as to whether or not your client will identify themselves. In the meantime, I have a sample of my mother's DNA and I've prepared the DNA testing kit in case we go forward. I am just concerned about the impact upon my parents should she not be who you are looking for.

"How do I reach you?" he asked.

"Please call me directly at 818.525.0333. Thank you, sir."

I'll be in touch, Miss Henderson. Thank you for your efforts. I hope we will be able to bring this to closure soon. I hope to speak to you within the next few days, goodbye." The gray-suited gentleman hung up.

"What's in it for them? Why would they willingly spend so much money to locate a lost relative just to give part of their wealth to? They must need something out of this." She was trying to cover all her bases. All those detective novels she was addicted to as a teenager were paying off.

Brit had a plan already in place. She was convinced that her mother did not have a clue about her adoption, and she couldn't risk the heartache of telling her unless Brit was sure of it. Brit had decided to tell her mother only after she had personally confirmed it.

The plan was to get a DNA sample of her buried grandparents and have it tested along with the requested DNA by the investigator.

Brit had an ex-boyfriend who was attending law school. The love-struck young man had not given up on his pursuit of her, still pined for her, and would do just about anything for her. She would ask for his help.

"I'll tell him that I have relatives who are trying to cheat me out of some inheritance from my grandparents and I need to secretly gather some DNA from them. It's at least part of the truth." She knew that would make him instantly protective of her.

"I'll ask him to create a fake court order for Forest Lawn Cemetery in order to have my grandparents exhumed, grab a DNA sample, and be off."

Exhumation was rarely done, but it could be accomplished. A rather simple alternative versus the drawn out legal requests allowed under California law, if there is a demonstrated legal necessity involved. Hers didn't fall under those parameters, but she would utilize them anyway.

This would put her on a clear path to understanding some of the clouded mysteries surrounding her mother's history. She figured, it was better to depend upon yourself for evidence rather than on a stranger's evidence. Who knows what alternative agendas those people might be hiding?

"I will prove once and for all if my mother was adopted, or not. As shattering as this kind of news could be, I know my mother is also a practical woman who deals with life head on."

Steering her second hand, old red convertible sports car up the long road to the massive, white stone entrance of Forest Lawn Cemetery-Hollywood Hills brought back memories of the death of her grandparents. She had been a little girl of 11 then, and it had been her first encounter with death. At the time, she felt it had helped that she understood that they were old, and had had a long life. They had loved her mother and her dearly. She was sure they would have approved of her actions. They had been the ultimate practitioners of practicality.

Brit took the fake subpoena to the cemetery office as requested. They needed a hard copy to go with the previously faxed one, and she paid the fee for the exhumation. It appeared, as she expected, that they were more interested in the fee than in the legal document. Having called ahead and arranged for the exhumation, the coffins were prepared in an enclosed tent for the sampling, and she was left alone.

Brit asked the attendant to collect the small hair samples as delicately as possible. She did not want to see the condition of the bodies. The coffins were closed. She kissed the coffins of her grandparents and stood quietly as they were returned to their resting place. Her fond memories of them gave her a strange calmness at having been this physically close to them again after all these years.

The DNA tests were sent off within two hours. It would take a week for the results. She could barely sleep wondering what the results would bring, more concerned about whether or not she was related to her grandparents than the strange lost relative issue at hand.

"Are our lives about to be turned upside down? Will I finally be able to put to rest the life-long mystery cloaking Mother's background, thus mine? If mother was adopted, who are her parents? Could they still be alive? And who were these mysterious people who have shown up out of nowhere with such keen interest in Mom's background?" She tossed and turned all night. Little did she know, those unsettling questions would be the least of her concerns over the next few days. Her life was about to change in ways that not even a Hollywood writer of fiction could have created.

Brit's mother would never learn of the results confirming whether or not she had been adopted, or if she was the lost relative of some, yet unknown, wealthy family.

Dotty Henderson was brutally murdered the following morning. The next few days became a nightmarish hell for Brit. No amount of good news could alter her grief and despair.

Chapter Twenty-Five

DETECTIVE GOLDMAN VS. AUNT MARJORIE

Rocco and Elsa sought out the surveillance video at Schwab's.

It captured a figure dressed in black wearing a hat and a knitted face mask. They'd entered the diner shortly after Dotty's arrival. It showed the same figure leaving after what must have been Dotty's murder. They found nothing on it that would assist in identifying the murderer. They couldn't tell if it was a woman or a man, nor did it give them any discernible behaviors or identifying characteristics.

However, they did discover the video of the visiting stranger in the gray suit no one seemed to be able to identify.

In the meantime, they had to interview Dotty's daughter to gather any information that might provide them with a lead.

Michael Deeves was willing and able to give almost detective-like details of the appearance and approximate times he had witnessed the well-dressed stranger who showed up at Schwab's one day out of the blue.

"I noticed him right away. He was impeccably dressed, and seemed to stare at Dotty in an unusual manner. I remember at one point I saw the man reach for a spoon with a handkerchief after Dotty had placed it on the counter. The man quickly removed his hand as Dotty was turning unexpectedly to face him," he proudly offered, using his most descriptive prose.

The two detectives identified the man who they would later interview.

It was now time to speak to Dotty's daughter Brit.

Brit Henderson was visibly shaken with grief and shock over the loss of her mother, but agreed to speak with them.

"I'll do anything I can to help find whoever did this to my mom."

"Miss Henderson, we are deeply sorry for your loss from the bottom of our hearts. We both knew your mother for many years as regulars at Schwab's. I want to assure you that we are taking this on a personal level, and will do everything within our power to find whoever did this," Elsa said as she tried to calm the grieving daughter.

"We'd like to find out a little bit about your mother's background if we may?" Rocco asked.

"Of course, whatever you need to know."

"Did you know of anyone who might have wanted to hurt your mother for any reason?"

"No. But I have seen all the nasty things in the papers they are saying about her. That was not the mother that I knew, I can tell you that. My mother never once indicated to me that she was doing anything like that. And, I simply don't believe she would. My mother cared for and respected everyone that I have ever seen her come into contact with, from the garbage men to the postman. That's just the way she was," Brit exclaimed.

"Had she or you met anyone recently that may have been out of the ordinary?" asked detective Goldman.

"Well, as a matter of fact yes. There was something odd that happened a few days ago. This strange, well-dressed man came to our house in the middle of the day looking for my mother. I was just about to leave for school, I'm a senior at UCLA."

"What did he look like, and what was he looking for?" Rocco asked.

Brit gave them a description.

Detective Goldman and Elsa looked at each other. Elsa pulled out a photograph from her breast pocket.

"Was this the man?" she asked Brit.

"That's him! I normally would never let a stranger into the house when I'm alone, but he seemed professional, well dressed, driving an expensive car, you know. He seemed OK. Besides, I pretended my boyfriend was upstairs, just in case, and I reminded him that he was on the home security camera. And since I was her daughter, I handled most of her personal business affairs. And I really do, just to help keep scammers away from my parents," she stated.

"Did he tell you what he wanted to speak to your mother about?" Rocco continued.

"Yes. He said that he was a lawyer. Some kind of investigator for someone who was searching for a lost relative and that they thought my mother might be that person. That he needed to verify whether she was or not. That there may be a large amount of money involved. Then he asked if I would ask mom for a DNA sample. It was all very strange," Brit said as she drifted in and out of tears.

"Did he tell you who his client was?" Elsa added.

"No, although I did ask. I was suspicious and tried to find out as much information as possible in case it was some kind of scam. I told him that I would have to have more information before disturbing my mother with something like this. I didn't want to bother her with what could be some kind of scam. The oddest thing about the whole experience was that he told me that my mother was adopted. I am absolutely sure my mom nor I knew this. She just would not have hidden something like this. And, she would have wanted to know who her parents were. I know my mom.

"So, before telling my mom about any of this, I asked her if she knew about any rich lost relatives. She said no and that was the end of our discussion. I did a little sleuthing on my own, intrigued with the adoption statement."

"Your mother is an only child I take it?"

"Yes, my grandparents died when I was a child so there weren't many relatives except for my Aunt Marjorie and her son George. In fact, I paid a visit to her when trying to find out any information about the family history."

"And did you find out anything that might be of any help?"

"Oh yes! My Aunt Marjorie is about 92 years old if I remember correctly. She is also not a woman who talks very much about the past. She told me something that might be of some value. My aunt told me that she had some private documents that were to be given to my mother only upon her death, and that these documents would shed some light on any questions about our family history."

"Documents about your mother's past?"

"I assumed so. She held the information about those documents as if the safety of the world depended on it. Wouldn't tell me a thing about them. I am sure they have something to do with my mother's real history."

"Why do you say, real history?"

"After the odd visit from the strange man in the gray suit, and my conversation with Aunt Marjorie, I snuck a DNA test from my mother. I found out that she was definitely adopted, 99% sure."

"Wouldn't you need the DNA of your grandparents for that?" inquired Elsa.

"Let's just say I was able to find what I needed and carried out the test."

This was getting more complicated by the minute. Rocco and Elsa looked at each other as if to say "Whoa!"

"Did you give this information to the gentleman seeking out your mother?"

"No. I only found out the day after mom was … killed," she said softly, through tears.

Elsa sat next to her and wrapped her arms around her to comfort her.

"In my last conversation with this stranger, I told him that we needed to know who his client was before having any further contact."

"Did he leave any contact information?" Rocco asked.

"Yes. Here, I'll give it to you."

Rocco and Elsa took the contact information from Brit for the stranger and thanked her for her time. They assured her that they would be getting back in touch with her to keep her updated on the progress. And they offered to speak to her at anytime if she needed someone to talk to. They both gave her a comforting hug and left.

"We need to talk to Mr … ." Elsa glanced down at the business card given to them by Brit,

"Mr. James D. Celletti, of Thurston, Summerfield & Celletti, Inc. A Law firm."

"We need to talk to Mr. Celletti and find out his game plan and what the fuck has he been up to, and for whom." Rocco shared with an edge of venom in his tone.

"Agreed!"

Rocco and Elsa were a well-oiled team, having spent five years together on the Hollywood Police Department's homicide force as partners. Rocco couldn't think of a better partner to be working with on what was turning out to be the biggest case in his career. He had tried to persuade Elsa to stay on the force but understood the concerns of her new wife. After all, that was why he was still single. His serious girlfriends just weren't the types to have their future husband dealing with murders every single day, along with the possible danger of him becoming a target.

They wanted this vicious murder of their old friend solved as fast as possible. Whoever did this to Dotty was a clear and present danger to the whole city.

* * *

Victoria thought it would be important to share this information with the detectives. It would clear the air and help verify Michael Deeves was not involved in the extortion and blackmail.

Cino sat quietly listening to what Victoria had just told him regarding the call from Michael Deeves. It gave him an sense of relief.

"When are the pictures going to be returned?" he stoically asked.

"As soon as the investigation is complete I think? In the meantime, Detective Rocco has assured me that they will remain under lock and key with access only allowed to him and his captain. He said that he would try to clear Michael before all of the information goes to the L.A. Prosecutor's office. That way he will be able to return them to us sooner."

"Great! Because I don't want private pictures of my "wife" floating around the world!"

"Your wife?" Victoria kind of giggled.

"My wife!" Repeating the words as he stood up, grabbed her by the waist, and lifted her up in the air.

"I want to marry you, Victoria Salvaggio! I want to make babies with you!"

"Si!" Victoria answered with a huge smile on her face.

"You are the one. The one fate had in store for me. I know that with all my heart!"

"And you for me, Cino Salvaggio!" Slowly kissing him as if it were the first time.

As worried as she was about the photos, she was convinced something good had come out of the bad experience. It definitely had brought them closer together, out of concern for each other.

He tenderly kissed both her hands and then slid his grandmother's ruby encrusted emerald engagement ring on her finger.

"I promised my Nonna that I would share this with the woman I marry. She insisted it would keep a part of her with me after she had gone. Now, it is that special moment for me to share this in life." He knelt on both his knees staring up at her face.

"It takes my breath away, amore! I will cherish it forever. I have never loved anyone like I love you, Cino," she told him through the tears streaming down her face.

"I will see to it that you never do, by being the best husband in the world my treasure." As he begins to cry as well.

"Let's get started on that first baby!" She began unbuttoning his shirt.

Chapter Twenty-Six

THE STANFORDS

Gossip has a way of turning smoke into fire.

In the beginning, there were rumors, but nothing more than slight whispers. No one was willing to offend a family who wielded the kind of power as did the Huntington-Stanfords. Especially if the rumors turned out to be true. Or, if one had their own secrets to protect.

Clay Stanford II's personal secretary had intercepted a rumor of a child having been secretly given up for adoption by his wife. The secretary had explored these rumors through his contacts with the staff of other socialites. If these rumors were true, Clay Stanford blamed himself. It was he who had selfishly left his young bride for long periods of time during which he indulged in ridiculous adventures around the world. He had to climb the highest mountain or sail the longest distances to feed his passion for living life on the edge. He never spoke of the rumor to his wife. He feared any speculation would entail adultery. Life without his beloved Gemma would be impossible, and death would have been a more compassionate alternative. Therefore, he left it alone.

He would, however, do all within his power to circumvent his wife while attempting to find out if a child did, in fact, exist. The thought of a child of his, or hers, out there in the world alone, without him to protect them, sickened him. It never occurred to him that the child might be living in a safe, loving home.

Clay II included in his will, "Shall a third child of mine or my wife's ever be confirmed, such child shall share equally in my entire estate along with any and all born or unborn siblings. The codicil shall be in effect for perpetuity."

In June of 1956, Clay Stanford II's passion for traveling around the world offered him a chance to persuade his wife, Gemma Huntington-Stanford, to join him on a grand tour of Europe for her birthday celebration. He had just purchased a new Italian villa and winery in Tuscany, as a birthday surprise.

They were to return home to California via New York a month later in July.

Arriving at the Italian port of Genoa, the Stanfords transferred to the most luxurious ocean liner in the world at the time, the Italian luxury liner *Andrea Doria,* along with their two children, son Montague and daughter Isabella. The ship continued on to stops in Cannes, France, Naples, and Gibraltar while collecting almost 1200 other passengers before commencing its 51st voyage westward across the Atlantic for New York City, United States.

The transatlantic crossing would end in tragedy. The magnificent *Andrea Doria* seamlessly glided across the Atlantic as one of the fastest ships of its time. Italy's industries had been devastated in World War II and the Italian State was looking to regain its position of prestige on the world stage. The *Andrea Doria* was its answer. It was postwar Italy's calling card to the world. Elegantly designed, and equipped with the latest in technology, it was the first ocean liner to sport three swimming pools. The sophisticated ship swaggered around the globe with a gross tonnage of 29,100 tons and a crew of 500.

Nearing the end of their journey and only a few days from New York City, they approached Nantucket, Massachusetts when tragedy leapt from the sea. On the fog-filled night of July 25, 1956, the *MS Stockholm* of the Swedish American Line and the *Andrea Doria* collided with a metal-crushing death grip. The *Andrea Doria* was pierced broadside at a 90-degree point by the *Stockholm*. The Swedish ship's bow was built with a sharply raked angle that also served as an ice breaker when en route to wintry Scandinavia. It tore straight into the mid-section of the *Andrea Dora* like a hot knife into butter.

The violent collision smashed deeply into three passenger cabins numbered 52, 54, and 56. The crash annihilated the occupied first class cabins of the Stanford family. They were killed instantly, except for Montague.

News reports declared "the death toll to be 46 passengers, all onboard the *Andrea Doria*. Those unfortunate souls were located in the collision area of the ship. Among the fatalities were billionaire Clay Stanford II, his wife, heiress Gemma Huntington-Stanford, and daughter Isabella. The Stanford's only son, by the grace of GOD, has survived. After the ships separated, crew members of the *Stockholm* were surveying the damage and looking for survivors when they found a young boy, lying on the deck of the *Stockholm*, aft of the wrecked bow. It was young Montague Romeo Stanford, shivering, wet, but alive and without any major injury."

It was soon determined that he had been an *Andrea Doria* passenger and identified. He had miraculously survived the impact and had been propelled far onto the *Stockholm*'s deck, only a foot or two from being thrown into the open seas. His sister Isabella who had been in cabin 52 with him, her bed just a few feet away, had perished instantly.

The disaster would be the last of the great ships built before air travel surpassed ocean liners as the preferred means of intercontinental travel.

Thus began a era that would change our planet forever, a time when flying became the primary mode of world travel. A period that was to be created, and globally dominated, by Pan American World Airways. An era helped ushered in by none other than son, Montague Stanford.

* * *

Gemma Huntington was an American blue blood. When she married Clay Stanford II it united two of the largest fortunes in America, creating a colossal sum of unimaginable wealth. She had lived an idyllic life of old California money, cut from a different cloth than East Coast heiresses, thus giving her zero interest in the constant shop and spend life so many of them had chosen to lead. Gemma preferred to focus on her new husband, art, and entertaining in her magnificent mansions of San Marino (Old Pasadena), Montecito (Santa Barbara), or their 150 ft. yacht, *Cosmos*, all within a day's drive. She couldn't tolerate the endless hours of being on an airplane. Hence her avoidance of partaking in trips.

Her wish was to become pregnant straightaway after the wedding, but not even the super rich can force pregnancy. It certainly wasn't because of a lack of interest on Clay's behalf. Her husband had brought out a high sex drive in her that matched his. She was more than capable of keeping up with him on a daily basis. Yet, no children for the first two years. Or so he thought.

Gemma's husband Clay was gone two to three months at a time. It hadn't bothered her much at first. But she had become lonely and accustomed to the daily passion they shared for each other. Clay certainly took care of his needs when away from his wife, albeit discreetly, as one could in those days.

She withdrew from the society party circuit after marriage, leaving her with just her servants and the occasional visit from relatives or friends. These long periods of isolation resulted in her spending months at a time with her chauffeur and body guard, Daniels.

He was strikingly handsome, powerfully built, and just happened to be black. The two grew closer and the inevitable took its course, with Gemma giving in to her lustful longing for the passionate sex her husband had introduced her to. Only this time it was with her handsome black chauffeur, Daniels. But this was America in the 1940's.

"It is terrifically lustful, deliciously taboo, passionate, and very satisfying," she would think to herself when alone.

"I've almost become addicted to you, but you understand that this is only for us to enjoy until my husband returns home," Gemma spoke in an exhausted, hushed voice while lying in Daniels' arms after an hour and a half of nonstop, sweat-filled sex one summer afternoon.

"Yes. I know. But, until then, I intend to enjoy it as much as you. I'm so turned on by the thought of no one knowing that I'm sexing up my beautiful, sexy, rich white boss," was Daniels' reply.

The torrid affair ensued with three months of relentless sex. Shortly after the return of her husband, Clay, and amid fears that he would somehow sense the unusual chemistry between the two of them, she reluctantly dismissed Daniels. He would be missed, but he also left with a tidy sum from her as a gift of their "special" friendship. Enough to start his own limousine company.

Her secret was safe and she resumed her sought-after passion with her beloved husband. They spent nearly a week in bed when he first returned, much to the delight of Clay. She was strikingly beautiful and he would have done anything for her.

Soon after, Clay was off on another jaunt for business. Just as Gemma was finding herself feeling unusually sick. It had started a few weeks after Clay's return and would come and go.

"I won't go, dear, if you want me to stay. I can delay the trip," Clay reminded his loving wife.

"I am fine, my love. I want you to go as long as you promise you will give me twice as long with you when you get back."

"I promise with all my heart. We still have baby making duties to fulfill!" he replied with a smile in her direction as he prepared to leave.

Never suspecting that she might in fact be pregnant. That was until the clear signs that all women come to know arrived. Normally, she would have been thrilled at the prospect, but she was suddenly gripped with enough fear that it made her feel as if she'd taken a nude dip in a frigid February Lake Tahoe.

"I'm pregnant! I know it." Quickly realizing that it could very well be the child of Daniels. Thoughts raced through her mind as she tried to make sense of the timing. It could either be Clay's or her black chauffeur lover's.

Gemma harbored no idiotic ideas of racism herself, but she felt unable to handle the definite ridicule and exile that she would surely face in 1940's racist America. "I have two choices, give the child up or an abortion and risk ruining my chances of ever having children again."

Her clothes became roomier over the next few weeks as she made arrangements for her decision. She isolated herself and discreetly located a woman who handled these kinds of issues for women of high society. Done with the utmost in secrecy of course. Taking a course of action required her to encourage her husband to travel, which he gladly appreciated and took full advantage of.

"Darling, I love when you come home with all of your adventure stories. I look forward to it. I want you to travel the world as long as you can, just come back to me. I am going off to a spa to rid myself of a few extra pounds and keep beautiful for my handsome husband."

She was able to split their time apart by timing his short returns for the first three months. New York became a convenient travel destination for her when speaking to him. Although she hadn't truly been there in almost three years.

"You know I don't mind a little weight; I love you just as you are." Fulfilling his role as the adoring husband, never dreaming that she would be hiding a pregnancy from him.

Marjorie Heresford only handled underground adoptions for the wealthy. It was a black market service she had been in for years. She asked no questions about the father or circumstances, her only concern was carrying out the wishes of her clients and maintaining their secret. Her livelihood depended on it. Prying could end it all.

Gemma disappeared for a period of time on an extended trip while her husband was off on an expedition climbing Mt. Everest.

She gave the baby up at birth, having made up her mind that she would not look at it or hold it for fear that the already strong bond between a mother and child would make it impossible to give up, regardless of its color. It was the worst day of her life. She grieved for months, and months grew into years until she had conceived her next child. The woman had been told not to divulge anything about the child to Gemma, and she hadn't.

"I don't even want to know the sex. I couldn't bare it," she stated to the woman with a tone of dread.

The baby went straight to a childless family with whom the woman was well acquainted. They weren't well off, but they were full of love and she was confident that they would raise the child with the same care and affection as if it were their own flesh.

That child would grow up, get married, and later become known as … Mrs. Dotty Henderson. It had not been the lovechild conceived by Gemma and her lover, the chauffeur, but was, in fact, the full blooded offspring of her husband, Clay Stanford II.

Only the old woman whom Dotty knew as "Aunt Marjorie" knew the secret that she was the child of heiress Gemma Huntington-Stanford.

"I don't get paid to ask questions. I'm the solution for those that come to me for help. I offer the utmost in confidentiality," she assured the heiress and those like her. She was proud of the service she provided. Everyone involved was saved from heartache and pain, this she truly believed.

"So I've been told. The hefty sum you've been paid should be more than enough for your services." She had wanted to set aside money for the child, but that would entail attachments that could surface down the road. She had been assured the baby would be safe and taken care of.

"You've been very generous. Know that the child will be well taken care of."

"Good … I, I don't want to know anything else … please," she pleaded, afraid that she would change her mind at any minute.

"Yes, madam, understood. That is usually the case. This process is part of the services I provide. You are in good hands. I have been doing this for ladies of society for many years, with not one disruption or revelation. If you know what I mean." Cryptically bragging about her professional standing and past successes.

The old lady had operated like a covert government program for the privileged, assuming, from past experience, that the socialite had gotten pregnant by someone other than her husband.

Dotty turned out to be the spitting image of her grandmother, Clay II's mother. She had been homely looking as well, but filthy rich, which alone had secured her betrothal to the dashing Clay Stanford I.

The secret history of the child was noted only on a few old, faded documents kept under lock and key. The old woman kept them hidden away in her home for decades.

Dotty never knew her true relationship to "Aunt Marjorie," or that she was adopted.

Growing up, she had pondered as to why she didn't resemble either of her parents but was readily assured that she took after her grandparents. Little did they know what an unknown truth that truly was.

Dotty Henderson had led a life in full pursuit of relentless greed, fed by envy, for naught. The irony was that it would be she—not the inhabitants of Sherman Oaks, Hollywood or other enclaves of the rich—that the world would envy.

Their envy stemmed from Dotty's posthumous vast fortune and blue-blooded lineage. She was worth billions and never knew it, or for that matter, would never be able to enjoy one penny of it. Fate had interceded and dealt a cruel hand to her. Perhaps it was punishment for all the wicked and merciless deeds she had perpetrated upon so many others. Or, it could have been her just reward for having made a pact with herself "to do whatever it takes to get what I want" over so many years.

A few of her victims, whose lives she had destroyed in her quest for money, had been the ones who enjoyed the last laugh. Many of them rejoiced while giving one last kick of dirt and a hurl of spit aimed at her permanent "holding station" at Forest Lawn Cemetery.

Dotty Huntington Stanford-Henderson, lost heiress to one of the greatest fortunes in American history, daughter to a lineage that was as aristocratic and financially supreme as some of the world's oldest monarchs. Dotty had been cheated in the worst possible way.

It was not as if she could have avoided it, it was in her DNA. That dark part of her character she unknowingly inherited from her notorious grandfather, Clay Stanford I. It was the ruthlessness that had helped build the vast fortune her biological family had enjoyed over the last two centuries. The overpowering, cold-hearted detachment was beyond her control. It was her breeding that had determined her destiny.

* * *

Montague R. Stanford had grown his family's fortune twofold through the years after the loss of his immediate family by establishing a shrewd business regimen.

He had inherited the combined fortunes of his parents as the sole surviving family member, an estimated $4.3 billion, in 1956 dollars. His mother's brother, an only uncle, led the charge against the *Stockholm*, of the Swedish American Lines, for the death of his only sister. It was found that the inexperienced on-duty bridge officer of the *Stockholm* had read the radar incorrectly, one of many mistakes made by both ships' crews, which, in turn, lead to the collision.

Montague's upbringing was taken up by his robber baron grandfather, Clay Stanford I. He was raised with a hands-on approach by his grandfather, probably more out of grief and fear after the loss of his only son than by necessity.

Montague became a proverbial chip off the old block, either because of his grandfather's merciless DNA or simply as a dedicated student. More than likely, it was the former.

He had married a lovely artist, an ex-hippy named "Cosima." She had changed her name from Ruby Smith in the early days of her 1960's San Francisco era. Cosima had been a protester during a sit in at one of Montague's companies. Having recognized him in a car as it was entering the gates of the company she boldly approached it with her large protest sign that read "WHY?" in dripping red paint used to emulate blood. She was shocked when the car stopped and Montague rolled down his window to speak with her.

"What does your sign mean?" he asked as his heart leapt from his chest after the large sign, which had been blocking Cosima's face, slowly came down, revealing the most gorgeous coral green eyes he had ever seen, set in what he believed to be the most beautiful female face on the planet.

"The pollution going into the bay, killing all the fish and birds!" Her rage quickly fading as Montague gave her his deadly, feigned look of boyish innocence and warmth. His dashing sun-kissed brown hair, bronze tanned face, and sparkling smile had caught her off guard and unarmed her.

"Are we really doing that?" he asked?

"Yes … don't you know that? I think it is your company, isn't it?" As she began to wonder if she had approached the right man.

"What is your name?" he replied.

"Cosima! And who might you be?" Defiantly answering.

"I am Montague Stanford. I guess I'm the bad guy, but I'm not really! What can I do to make amends? Will you meet with me and discuss this? I don't want to hurt the little fish and birds," he responded.

"Are you serious?" Not knowing if he was making a joke of her or not.

"I am very serious! How about this evening? And you can tell all of your protesting friends that I will take your advice under consideration when implementing these changes," he challenged.

"Well. OK, if you are really serious!"

"Where can I reach you?" Replying with a boyish sincerity.

They met, the pheromones exploded, and they were married two months later! Clay Stanford III was born seven months later. He was an only child, though it certainly wasn't for lack of trying. The heat between Montague and Cosima made them inseparable. They had never traveled apart since their first meeting. At times, people just know from their first meeting, when they first lay eyes on each other, that they've found the one. That was the case between them. The pollution that was spilling out from his company was halted immediately.

* * *

Clay III had seen his grandfather's irrevocable trust containing the codicil that referred to a possible existence of a lost daughter. His father Montague was obliged to follow it. It could very well have been nothing more than a rumor. The Will or Trust also stipulated that an ongoing search was to be directly funded and verified by the legal oversight of his executors. His father had never discussed with him the possibility of a lost sibling.

There was recent news that made the possibility of his father having a sibling rise to the level of serious plausibility. It was becoming more real by the day with the advances of new medical technology such as DNA testing.

Being an only child, Clay III was to be crowned sole heir to a fortune of billions. He had no intention of sharing what he viewed as his multi-billion-dollar fortune with a complete stranger, regardless of their relationship. A person no one knew anything about.

Like his great grandfather, Clay I, he held dear the teachings of his father when it came to business and protecting the family's assets. The only difference was, in the current generation, Clay III had that extra bite of a "take no prisoners" ethic. Similar to his robber baron great grandfather. He had missed out on knowing his great grandfather so he hung onto every word and lesson his father shared with him as the gospel.

Clay III had been asked by his father, Montague, to embark upon a project in preparation for his responsibility of overseeing the vast fortune he was to inherit.

The task was to select a company owned by the family and improve its revenue over the course of a year.

"I'll leave it up to you to choose which industry you'd like to work with," he told his son.

Clay chose a successful construction company headquartered in California. Delving into its business prospects, he discovered that "Castle Industries" was to bid on a $1.1-billion-dollar State building project that oversaw the construction of the new high-speed train stations throughout the state. It would stretch from San Francisco to San Diego. It was massive. And it was the most ambitious high-speed project in the nation. Others were to follow across the nation.

Clay chose this project for several reasons. One, he was intrigued with the necessary lobbying aspect of it. Secondly, if he succeeded, it would position the company as the up and coming leader for similar projects in development across the nation. Thirdly, he wanted to impress his father. No easy task knowing the level of expectation Montague Stanford held for his only son.

Clay felt that he was up for the challenge. He was young, he was ambitious, and, most importantly, he was an exceptional student of his father's acumen when it came to learning how to listen.

"I will do this, and I will succeed!" he reassured himself. He lacked a few things in his development, but confidence was not one of them.

Clay met the following day to give his father his decision. He hadn't wanted to wait until the following week as his father had suggested. He wanted to display initiative and decisiveness.

"Pop, I've chosen Castle Industries! They are bidding on the high-speed rail stations throughout the state. I believe … no, I know, that I can take this and win. I'm ready for this," he boldly declared to his proud father.

"OK, son, it's yours. I'll set it up this week. Understand that this is a huge endeavor, opportunity, and potential disaster all rolled up into one. I will not hold it against you if it does not work out. Your dedication is what I will be observing." Montague wanted to give his son a way out should he fail.

Clay understood full well the seriousness of this opportunity.

He thought about his upbringing where failure was unacceptable in this family, and had never been rewarded or forgiven, he remembered.

"We have never been rewarded for second place, and I don't intend to be the first to be!"

He knew the rules of the game and was prepared to play. The stakes were enormous. He looked at his dad with powerful intensity.

"Thank you, Dad, I won't let you down." He had the weight of almost 175 years upon his shoulders. This was not England, Italy, Germany, or France, it was America and they play hard here. Clay's mind was already well at work developing his strategy.

He set out to find background dirt on the politicians.

"I am going to relish this. I'm going to compete and win, legally, of course. At least under the laws of the U.S.A.," Clay thought to himself.

Montague smiled as his son walked away. He saw himself in every inch of his son. He had no doubt that he would be as successful as he had been.

"I only hope that he remembers to be honest, and fair to all." A humble lesson he had learned as a young man. Never forgetting how his entire family was snatched from him in an instant with the unexpected sinking of the *Andrea Doria*, he always thought twice about stirring up bad karma.

That afternoon, Clay notified his personal assistant of a priority project that they would be embarking upon.

"This requires the ultimate in secrecy, dedication, and no questions asked. This is a serious business adventure and I need you to understand that this will take priority over everything in your life right now. I'm in this to win, and your job depends upon it. Are we clear about that? I reiterate to you that I am only interested in and expect solutions.

"You'll need some help so make sure your assistant is aware of the high level of importance placed on this project. He will be working with confidential information. I'll brief you further on the strategy after meeting with the heads of the company involved. In the meantime, find out which politicians are on the approval committee for the state high-speed rail stations. Then research full bios, both the official one and the hidden one." He set out to equip himself with as much dirt as he could in order to out-maneuver his competitors.

"Check," was his assistance reply.

Clay ended the conversation with, "You've performed well while working for me over the last two years, and you've been rewarded handsomely. I hope I can continue to depend on your discretion." He delivered the thank you as a veiled threat.

"Let's get busy!" He gave his assistant a devilish smile as he was leaving the room.

The connections he had set up with the college-aged sons of the two state politicians fell into place. Clay used every opportunity to spend time with his two new pals, and more importantly, their fathers. They, along with their wives and sons, would be invited to the Stanford's Emerald Ball, the most sought after social event of the year.

It helped that the three attended the same university.

Neither of the sons gave it a second thought when presented with the privilege of calling Clay Stanford III a friend. Nor were they opposed to the benefits that came with his family's immense wealth. The five of them jetted to and fro to attend openings and sporting events with front row seats of course, in Hawaii, San Francisco, New York, you name it. All on one of the family's private jets. Clay made sure they didn't spend a dime.

At first the fathers protested Clay's generosity, but their protests became more and more faint as the adventures became bigger and more extravagant, until the objections became nonexistent.

By the time Clay had invited their families to the Emerald Ball they were old friends. He had them exactly where he wanted them. He grew more confident by the day with his plan.

Chapter Twenty-Seven

STRANGER IDENTIFIED

"What exactly were you looking for during your visits to Schwab's, and why all the attention to Dotty?" was the first question Elsa asked of the stranger, who had now been identified as an attorney for a high-powered Hollywood law firm.

"I was hired by a client to verify whether or not Dotty Henderson was a lost relative. Someone my client's family has been searching for a very long time. Previous attempts had left enough information for me to narrow it down to Mrs. Henderson," Mr. Celletti replied.

"Why didn't you just come right out and let her know?"

"I was given very specific instructions on how to proceed. I was not to tip my hat to her in any way. She was not to find out in case she turned out not to be the person we were searching for. He thought it would avoid publicity that way."

"So, it is a he? And how did you intend to verify this?" Elsa pointed out.

"I was simply trying to discreetly collect a sample of Mrs. Henderson's DNA. The problem was, she was like a hawk watching my every move. I even tried to snag one of her coffee mugs, but she wasn't having it. She caught me every time. Apparently, the Schwab's mugs were a favorite souvenir item with certain visitors who would steal them in lieu of buying one. She caught me twice trying to sneak one of the ones she had handled. And she warned me, 'Third time and I call the cops.' I told her it was my mistake, just that the coffee was so good I forgot it was in my hand. That was the last time I visited Schwab's."

"So you switched to visiting her home in the middle of the day? When you assumed no one would be home?"

"Seems like you have done your homework."

"And then some," Rocco said dryly. "What were you doing at Mrs. Henderson's home in the middle of the day when you knew she would be at work?"

"I knew she had a daughter, I just figured that I could speak to her and maybe swipe a pen or pencil while chatting her up. Well, she was as sharp as her mother. Never took her eyes off me, not even when yelling up the stairs to her boyfriend," he told Rocco

"Who is your client sir?" Rocco cutting straight to the point.

"Come on, you know that I can't tell you that. That would be the end of my career in this business and this town." Half pleading with the officer.

"OK. Look, we can do this the easy way or the hard way. The hard way is you refuse to tell us now, and I turn your name and involvement over to the tabloids and newspapers as fresh red meat. That way, I'll just let their vicious hounds out on whoever your client is and they'll be under a cloud of suspicion and relentless publicity. That'll go over nicely with your future clients, if you can find any. How's that working for ya?" Rocco was proud of himself for strong arming the guy without having to touch him.

"Or … you can give us the information we need and we pretend we never had this conversation. Your client will be none the wiser. We'll find out anyway, and it'll save us from charging you with criminal obstruction and then serving you with a subpoena. Do I need to keep going? Cause I have a few other cards up my sleeve for you if need be." Rocco waited.

"You're good, and I am wise enough to recognize the better hand dealt. It was a member of the Stanford family that hired me," he answered, while waiting for the shocked response.

"Which one?"

"Clay III, the son. I was only hired to locate Mrs. Henderson and discreetly verify whether or not she was a missing family member they had been looking for."

"This is getting interesting. Did you know if his father was aware of this fishing expedition?"

"That I couldn't tell you. He paid me very, very well, and offered no additional information. When you've been in this business for as long as I have, you don't ask too many questions, you just listen and do what is asked. Then return with answers. These types of people are only interested in solutions and answers. They aren't interested in excuses."

"I met the daughter, explained everything to her without telling her the details, like who the family was, and asked for her help. I told her it could be of great benefit to her mother if we could prove her identity through a DNA test."

"And she agreed to help you? A stranger that she knew nothing about?"

"Well, it wasn't quite that simple. We communicated a bit, you know, and I gave her some details so that she would know that I was on the level, like sharing with her that I knew that her mother was adopted. She pretended not to be shocked, but I knew that neither Dotty nor her daughter were aware of that big secret."

"Thank you, you've been very helpful. I won't forget." Rocco started to leave.

"Thank you Detective Goldman. By the way, I am truly sorry about the tragedy that happened to that poor woman.

That horrible thing, right before discovering you are a member of one of the wealthiest families in America."

"Excuse me? So, you confirmed the DNA test?" Rocco stopped dead in his tracks as he was about to leave.

"Yes. This is strictly confidential, Detective. I intercepted the results that her daughter had submitted a few days before Mrs. Henderson's murder. She used a DNA kit that I had provided her during our meeting at her home. That kit carried an embedded alert that notified me whenever it was submitted. The sample was to come directly to my office, and if it was positive, I was instructed to send Mrs. Henderson one that had a negative result. I cannot speculate beyond that, Detective." The lawyer now shifted into self-preservation mode.

"Did you turn the real results over to your client?"

"I did."

"And?"

"That was the end of our business. He thanked me and that was it, case closed. I have no further information regarding this."

"You've just been awarded a free "get out of jail card" for that last piece of information, Mr. Celletti. Thanks." Rocco could barely contain himself as he left the building to call Elsa.

* * *

The investigator in the gray suit, Mr. Celletti, phoned Clay III immediately to inform him of the visit from Hollywood PD.

"I am very sorry, Mr. Stanford, they forced me to reveal the identity of my client."

"Not a problem, I'm sure they would have found out eventually. Thank you for notifying me. Did you give them any other information?"

"If you mean the DNA results, no. Thanks to your generous expense account, I used it to bribe the testing site employee.

She didn't blink an eye after seeing the $2500 dollars I offered her." Celletti replied.

"Excellent."

Mr. Celletti was smart enough to know that he had to protect himself on both flanks when dealing with both Clay and the police. "I didn't physically give him the results, but I didn't say that I did not tell him the results either." Celletti thought to himself while relishing his lawyering skills as he tried to shield the truth.

"If you don't mind me asking, Did the test results answer the question you were asking?" Celletti asked Clay III.

"You were paid for answers, not questions. Thank you for your services. I would hope that no further information might come from you should you be questioned at a later date. At this point, you should direct them to me. Is that clear?"

"Happy to. It's been a pleasure doing business with you, Mr. Stanford."

Clay had confirmed six months prior that Dotty Henderson was not related to the people who had raised her. He had also confiscated a strand of his father's hair from a brush in his dressing room. The match was 99.9%. He had finally found his father's missing sister. He had needed to hire this investigator to conceal his previous activities regarding Dotty Henderson. The detailed report informed him of Dotty's secret side job she was operating while working her day job as a waitress at that Hollywood diner, Schwab's. The information he received contained pictures of her morning sexual romps with Sam O'Brien, her boss at the diner, her bank account amounts, and a list of people whose lives had been most damaged by her secret snitching to the tabloids for profit.

* * *

Rocco asked Elsa if she would do him a favor and handle the follow-up questioning of the Tripartite. His plate was too full to add those three divas to it.

"In the meantime, I'm going to pay 'Aunt Marjorie' a visit."

He headed north on Vermont in the direction of Los Feliz.

"This probably won't take very long. Then I can grab a bit of lunch, I'm starved."

He knocked on the old lady's door and waited for an answer. He heard light footsteps approaching the front door.

"Yes, who is it?" a feeble voice asked.

"Hello, ma'am, I'm with the Hollywood Police Department. My name is Detective Rocco Goldman, I'm sorry to disturb you at this time so soon after your loss." He flashed his badge at the glass panel the old lady was staring out of. He started to put his badge away.

"Hold it up for a while longer, so that I may see it more clearly." She peered closer at the badge while opening the curtains a little wider, exposing her small four-foot frame.

"OK, sir. Just a minute." Cracking the door far enough for Rocco to get a glimpse of that notorious raised-eyebrows look of suspicion. The one she always delivered to unknown visitors after opening the door.

"Ma'am, I'm here to ask some questions about your deceased niece, Dotty Henderson. I am sorry for your loss, my condolences."

The old lady took a deep sigh and held her handkerchief to her nose while sniffling and shaking her head.

"I still can't believe that child is gone. She was such a lovely child."

"I understand you were her only relative outside of her daughter and husband?" he asked.

"There's George, my son. But Doty and I weren't really blood related. I have been in her life since her birth. Those are the ones that are important in life," she added.

"I see. Thank you for telling me that. What I'd like to know, ma'am, is, Do you have any information or documents pertaining to her biological relatives?"

She stiffened up and stared directly at him. "Why would you ask me something like that?"

"It's normal procedure in a case like this."

"Maybe you had better come in. And, will this information … if there is any, be made known to the public?"

"I can't say, ma'am. I can tell you that I will do all that I can to respect your wishes. But I just can't guarantee anything in a murder investigation."

"Well, I do have some information that I promised long ago not to reveal to anyone. I was going to give it to Dotty upon my death."

"May I see it?"

"Am I required to show you by law?" she asked suspiciously.

"No, ma'am, not right now. But if I don't see them now, I'll be forced to legally order you to. And I don't want to have to go that route with you, not with your recent loss and Dotty's family still grieving. Then you'll have newspapers all over your home, day and night. It will just turn into a mess with you smack in the middle of it. Do you understand?" Try to inform her as delicately as he could.

"Yes, sonny, I guess I do. This stuff is a bit too much for an old lady like me to handle … I'll be 93 in a few months. I just hope it doesn't stir up too much after all these years. I'm so upset over losing Dotty. I don't know if I could handle much more," she pleaded.

"I will do what I can to protect you, and Dotty's family. I knew her personally as a friend from Schwab's, where she worked," he shared.

"Oh, I know of that place. It's where that movie star Lana Darnell hangs out I believe. Dotty took me there once years ago, in 1981, for lunch. I tell you, I was expecting Miss Swanson to come through those doors any minute. It was just full of those movie types. I have such fond memories of my little Dotty. She's the only one who stayed in touch with me you know."

"What do you mean the only one? Where their other siblings?"

"Oh excuse me, I'm just mumbling."

What she had accidentally let slip out was her secret profession of underground black market adoptions and the children she provided. For some reason, she had stayed involved in Dotty's life versus the others.

The old lady stood up and hobbled over to the fireplace, glanced over her back at Rocco as if to make sure he was a real policeman. Quickly deciding that he was legit.

"I'm only doing this to help my poor Dotty you know." She half spoke and half mumbled mixed with a sniffle or two of genuine grief.

"I know you are, ma'am. It is very much appreciated and it may help us in finding whoever did this," he reassured her.

With that, she placed her hand on the third corner brick down from the fireplace's mantle and gave it a slight shove. There was a small click and out popped the brick. It swung open as if attached to a hidden hinge. Rocco could clearly see there was a good deal of space hidden in there, enough that the old lady could almost reach her whole arm in. She slowly pulled out a large, old envelope. One that was so old it had turned the yellowish color of aged paper.

"Will you need to take them with you? I'd prefer you look at them here and leave them with me."

"I can do that, ma'am." He was practically panting with anticipation.

"Be very careful, sonny, they are pretty darn old, like me!" she told him before releasing them into Rocco's hands.

He almost tore the damn thing right then and there before slowing down. Uncurling what appeared to be a letter and several documents, he began to read.

"Oh my dear sweet Jesus!" Right there in front of him was documented proof that Dotty Henderson was the biological child of Gemma Huntington Stanford and Clay Stanford II! This was incredible! This explained the young Clay Stanford's involvement, and the mysterious investigator in the gray suit.

"So, now you know," the old lady said quietly with her small framed little body engulfed in her big overstuffed chair as she stared straight ahead into the crackling fire.

"She tried to give me a false name at first, but I always did my homework, for the benefit of the children, you know. She hadn't even wanted to look at the child. I found out why later on. You see, back in those days we had our connections through the servants. We knew pretty much everything before these ladies even got to us. Nothing got past the servants."

Rocco was floored. He couldn't believe his ears. He was afraid to interrupt the old lady with any questions. He wanted her to sing until she couldn't sing anymore.

"It was pretty much the usual in those cases. What I mean is, those poor young things, with all their money, would be left alone by gallivanting husbands, locked away in those great big ol' mansions with just their servants until they returned. They'd get lonely. They'd spend too much time with the manservant, and you know, those things would just happen.

"In Mrs. Stanford's case, it was with the chauffeur ... it was always the chauffeur or groundskeeper. They'd either keep the child and pass them off as their husband's or pay a visit to me and I'd handle the situation for them. Something women like me have been handling for hundreds, if not thousands, of years for the rich.

"The only problem this time was Mrs. Stanford's chauffeur happened to be colored! A fine looking, big strapping man from what I heard. I wasn't of the type to judge people on color as most whites did in those days. Didn't believe in it. I'm a Quaker, descended from staunch abolitionists. Couldn't stand how those poor people were treated. Truth be told, I think we all have a bit of coffee in us." Stopping for a moment to give herself a little chuckle.

"Well, she told me she didn't want to see the child because it might make her change her mind about giving it up. I think she was afraid that it might be born colored. Well, it wasn't. It was white, as white as a white child could be born white. I suspected and later confirmed it was Mr. Stanford's child, as the servants knew for a fact that there had only been two men with that woman, one white and the other black. That meant Dotty's father was Clay Stanford II.

"Well, I'm done. I've wanted to get that off my conscience for many, many years," she sighed and exhaled.

For the first time in Rocco's life, he was speechless. He literally could not mouth one word.

The old lady moved her glare from the fire over to him after a moment of silence and spoke again.

"Lord knows it is a story that would cause an earthquake back in those days. I'd wanted to tell Dotty her whole life, but Rose and Stanley had been so good to her. Loved her from the time I placed her in their arms. I just didn't know what to do, I didn't want to hurt anyone. So, I just kept my mouth shut all these years."

Rocco could see the small tears beginning to flow down her winkled cheeks, emanating from the blank stare focused on the flickering flames of the warm fire.

He rose from his chair and walked over to her, leaned down and hugged her.

"You did the right thing. There really was nothing else you could have done. I understand now why you had such a connection to Dotty. You have my deepest respect, ma'am. Please know that." As tough as he was, holding her small little frail body in his arms made him choke up. She had carried the weight of the world on her little frail shoulders. All in the name of helping others.

Aunt Marjorie broke down crying in Rocco's hug, held onto his arms with her tiny little hands. Something he felt she had wanted to do for decades. To ease the burden of so many secrets, this one in particular. He told her he would make a point of staying in touch with her. She thanked him and bid farewell.

Chapter Twenty-Eight

EMERALD BALL

The Emerald Ball was a high-profile yearly event that celebrated sustainable development with clean water and air technologies, while helping to reduce humanity's carbon footprint. It was one of the most sought after invitations of the year, and attendance was closely held to a highly selective guest list of 200 people from around the world. At the top of the guest list was the President and First Lady of the United States of America.

No matter how important you were or thought you were, the Emerald Ball was strictly invitation only.

Every year, this being Hollywood, one would hear the inevitable, "Do you know who I am!" from someone showing up without an invitation. They are shocked to hear the level-headed, stern guest concierge Mrs. Betty Joan Winters reply, "Sir, Miss, we've turned away senators, movie stars, and royalty who've shown up uninvited. There have not, nor will be, any exceptions. Thank you, please step aside."

The only exception ever made was five years earlier when an uninvited Russian billionaire arrived who was told he could not enter without an invite. He apologized then asked if he could make an on the spot donation of $200,000 dollars for this great cause. He was instantly put on the guest list from that point forward.

The hosts for the event were Mr. Mrs. Montague and Cosima Stanford. In the beginning it was more Montague indulging Cosima than a sincere interest of his. However, it grew into a spectacular international event that he was extremely proud of. Even he was amused by the intrigue that occurred in a room with such a concentration of global power and fame. The exclusivity created a ferocious battle for the elites attempting to climb the social ladder.

It was an evening filled with high-profile networking with A list movie stars holding court over the global super rich, with the power of leading politicians thrown in for spice.

It marked Cino's first night out into the Hollywood spotlight with glamorous Victoria Steele, CEO of American International Films. He had made it clear to Victoria that he had zero interest in Hollywood parties. He did, however, relish a certain amount of excitement and exhibitionism at the chance to show off his beautiful, sexy lover on his arm. And she was exhilarated at the thought of women drooling over her smoldering lover.

Victoria was a little anxious at the thought of introducing him to her world for a number of reasons. One, she was rightfully weary of the "she wolves" of Hollywood laying their eyes on him. They were dangerous competition for any woman, but especially for one with arguably the most handsome man in town. Secondly, she struggled to admit it, but she was hesitant to introduce her new fiancé.

The idea of it carried all sorts of connotations.

"I'll deal with it later." Thinking aloud to herself.

He wasn't too keen on going one way or the other. He had had his fair share of jet set parties in the capitals of Europe. He'd attend for her.

"I don't mind going, it's just that most of those people are boring," he replied to Victoria after she pleaded with him to accompany her.

"I'm not interested in climbing the hill in Hollywood, acting, or bed hopping," he told her.

His reply made her feel even more secure in their relationship.

"He is strangely real," was how she described him to herself.

"How bizarre it is when I find that there are people in the world who could give a damn about movies, and all the baggage that comes with fame and wealth," she reminded herself of her shifting perspective of the world.

The party had attendees from as far away as Manhattan, Tokyo, London, Saudi Arabia, Cape town … .

In keeping with the theme of the event, all lighting was provided by solar energy, the unused food donated to food banks.

Champagne flowed like an endless river, and several chefs from top restaurants in Los Angeles and Rome created the dinner.

The Stanford estate was an extraordinary California Mission Style villa designed and built by the famous Californian architect Paul Williams. The forward part of the home wrapped around a gigantic swimming pool with gardens imitating those of ancient Roman villas. The back of the massive living room opened directly to the outside with disappearing walls.

It was January 29th, a few days after a torrential downpour that had left two inches of liquid life for Mother Earth to absorb, and everything in the garden looked lush and inviting. The infamous Wolf Moon appeared on the January 29th, the night of the Emerald Ball. The term is from a Native American legend that speaks of hungry wolf packs howling outside of their villages for thousands of years. It is also known as the "Old Moon." The "wolves of Hollywood" pay significant homage to both definitions.

Everyone knew that this party would be packed with some of the fiercest wolves in Filmdom, howling to the full moon and dripping in Hollywood glamour. The effects of the "Wolf Moon's" gravitational pull mixed with the finest Californian and French champagne created an unpredictable evening.

Cino and Victoria drove up the long driveway towards the entrance of the mansion. The long winding drive was lined with Maserati, Cadillacs, Rolls Royce's, Jaguars, and every other expensive car in the world.

The front of the villa was lit from the ground up, casting it in a movie set style appearance. White vested, white gloved valet attendants, all handsome young men from local universities, lined the entrance to the villa on both sides of the driveway.

"Well, we're here. Here goes! Let's have some fun, honey!" She was excited to show her future husband off to the world.

Victoria first extended her long arm out of the car for the valet.

Wearing $250,000 dollars of the purest, deep green emeralds, also known in the ancient world as gems of Venus, Goddess of Love, Victoria Steele rose from the Jaguar wearing a body hugging, 1930's era shimmering gold satin gown that fit like a painted-on glove. The contrast of the emeralds against the gown, and her breathtaking beauty, made her look like a dream. She made a point of holding her hand up to gather her satin shoulder wrap, exposing her to-die-for engagement ring as the cameras flashed nonstop.

Cino couldn't keep her eyes off her, which made the drive to the party a challenge. He had told her during their drive up the long driveway, "I want this evening to be over already."

"It won't be that bad, my love, I promise," she answered, while staring at his profile in the light of the car's interior.

"Its just that … it's very difficult for me to look at you now, as beautiful as you are, without wanting to devour you on the spot," he said with a passionate tone of seriousness.

"I love you and I will prove it to you at home when I do your favorite slow dance as my dress falls." Leaning over to plant a kiss on his cheek.

He valiantly tried to catch her kiss on his lips while almost running the car into the bushes lining the driveway.

They made their way through the crowded grand room. It was packed with every major star of film, TV, and music in what seemed like the world. All of whom were clearly aware of who had just arrived.

Victoria Steele and her new Italian lover, the soon to be husband and father of her babies.

The wave of power wattage rolled through the room as everyone's eyes slowly and discreetly followed her and Cino. They headed to the open area by the pool, garden, and bar.

The couple, who brought with them a combination of extraordinary looks and style, stepped outside where the pool and cabana unfolded beneath them. They momentarily stopped at the top of the stairs to witness up and coming starlet Summer Lovejoy rising out of the pool with steam floating off of her black strapless wet gown and reaching for a glass of champagne and a towel from a handsome waiter standing nearby. Flashes from the authorized photographers lit up the area like blinding movie premieres.

Summer had taken a dip in the pool up to her neck, making sure her make-up and hair remained in movie-set perfection. She was stunning and clever enough to know that her little dip caught the eye of every producer, director, and billionaire within in eyesight. The women stared with bitchy envy at her daring maneuver. The wet dress had clearly outlined her vivacious body.

"I guess that was enough for them to remember my name." Giggling to herself while throwing her head back in a dramatic pose for the cameras.

"I can't wait to tell Gavin. God, I am so thankful for that hunk of a good-hearted man." Wondering how he had managed the incredible trick of snagging an invite.

She only wished he had been there to see her work her stuff, and be on his arm. Summer had learned not to ask too many questions when he delivered the impossible, discreetly and without seeking any overwhelming response from her.

"This is for you, my love. I want you to be there, it will be an important step in your career," he had said before dropping her backwards in his arms and planting a deep kiss on her lips.

Gavin had received the invite from a Broadway producer, one of his regular clients. The producer had become quite attached to Gavin over the three years since they'd met. He'd introduced him as his "trainer." Everyone in L.A. has a trainer, it's just that most don't provide the full range of services, as did Gavin.

The producer had to be in New York and offered it to Gavin as a tip along with his usual fee of $5000. Gavin was more than happy to accept and showed his appreciation by giving his client a few extra hours of fun, "for the road, good friend" was all he said as the sound of a zipper made itself known in the silent room.

Gavin's ability to call upon his persona of cool corporate detachment reflected his disdain for fake moral conventionality. He was true to only one rule, "Be true to thyself and those you love." He would have been a fantastic actor, no doubt. He's ability to assume the role of temporary lover to his clients was Oscar worthy.

* * *

One flash was all it took for the wave of attention to swiftly redirect towards Victoria and Cino. The image of the striking pair at the top of the stairs was priceless. The camera flashes took on the life of a solar flare as the pair descended the stairs to the pool and garden.

It was a sight of classic Hollywood glamour at its finest. Two of the most attractive people in this town, backed up with unrivaled movie industry power. Real power, the kind that translated into billions of dollars in movie-making revenue.

Victoria whispered into Cino's ear, "I'm sorry for this, darling, please don't be upset. I wasn't expecting anything like this. I'm sure your handsomeness is partially to blame."

"Ha, I hardly think so, standing next to you. I'm sure I am invisible to these people. You are more stunning than all of those emeralds around your beautiful neck combined."

He did his best to deflect all of the attention towards Victoria, but it was useless, it was the sight of the two of them together that fed the frenzy. He slyly smiled at her while attempting to lean over and kiss her, just as the camera flashes took it up another notch. One would have thought that was impossible from the blaring flashes. He knew then and there that he had to watch his every move in public when he was with his lover. Otherwise, the scene would be splashed around the world within minutes.

The two of them gracefully descended the stairs and were met by none other than Cosima and Montague Stanford at the bottom, something the hosts had never done for anyone, except the President and First Lady of the United States.

This was an exception, and the reaction of the press was unbelievable. The quintessential, visually breathtaking Hollywood couple had arrived.

Summer was not amused.

She was, however, clever enough to know and understand her current station in the pecking order of this town. She would observe, learn, and prepare for her day in the future when it would be she who commanded that kind of power.

* * *

Clay III had become friends with two sons of his targeted politicians. He had ensured that they, along with their fathers and mothers, were invited to the event, knowing full well that neither of them would refuse.

He positioned himself where it would be impossible for the group to walk past without seeing him and the famous crowd surrounding him. He waited, and monitored with his peripheral vision the strategic moment to acknowledge his young friends when they neared him.

Clay pretended to nonchalantly turn away from the crowd of famous faces that had engulfed him so as to face his new friends by coincidence.

"Tom, Mike! How are you!" he yelled as he excused himself from the circle and moved towards his two friends.

"Clay! Hey there, buddy! Oh my gosh, man, this is so incredible! Tom Willis, son of Congressman Mark Willis, excitedly replied.

"Please meet my mother and father, Martha Willis and Congressman Mark Willis," Tom extended.

"Congressman and Mrs. Willis, the pleasure is all mine. I'm very pleased the both of you could make it tonight. As you can see, quite a few of your supporters are here. It is for a great cause and we hope to raise a lot of money and awareness tonight."

"Thank you, Clay, for the kind invite tonight. It was very generous for you to extend this to my family," said the congressman as he extended his hand to Clay.

"Mike, this must be your mom and dad, Mrs. Masters and Senator Masters?"

"Yes, Mom, Dad, may I introduce Clay Stanford III?" Mike said as he formally presented his parents to Clay.

"My goodness, Clay, it's just a delight to be here! Please thank your parents for us," the pretentious Mrs. Masters said. She couldn't believe that she was actually there.

"Now this is how a U.S. Senator's wife should live. I've got to make sure my husband doesn't blow this connection as much as he hates networking," Mrs. Masters thought to herself as she looked around the room.

"I would love to, but I hope that you will be able to do that yourselves if I can locate them. I told my parents that you would be here tonight," he replied.

"Thank you, Clay," Senator Masters replied with a big smile.

"Please help yourselves to some dinner and refreshments. I'll be right back after I locate mom and dad." Clay had no intention of running after his parents. He would work on getting the two politicians alone in the library and shower them with praise.

* * *

"My father had grown the family fortune twofold in his lifetime, and, at the very least, I intend to double it again under my watch!" he vowed to himself.

Montague never inquired about his progress except to tell his son that he was there for him should he need him. Thoroughly impressed with his son's success, he escalated his son's responsibilities. Clay III had learned well.

He had coffee with his two new pals and offered them a proposition too good to be true. He asked for that they get their dads on the phone as he wanted to include them.

"Listen, guys, I'd like to share something really special with you. We've become pretty good pals over the last three months and I think its time I shared with you a sort of a "big league party."

"Firstly, to you, Senator, and Congressman, Dad and I would like to extend our support to both of you in your reelection campaigns!"

"Why thank you, Clay, and please extend my thanks to your father for me," said Senator Masters.

"That goes for me as well, Clay." echoed the congressman.

"I also wanted to extend an invitation for all of you to join me on a quick jaunt to Monte Carlo for four days as my guests. We can mix a little fun with some sightseeing, food, and a few spin at the tables. My dad will be joining us later there." He'd timed it so neither of the sons would be available to go as a result of finals. It was only important for the fathers to join him … and, no, his father would not actually be joining them. This was a ruse.

The two sons protested in vain that they would miss the trip because of school commitments. There was no way they could get out of them.

"That's too bad, guys. Just remember though, the three of us have a few months of summer to play before diving into big professions!" Clay tried to ease the sons' disappointment.

"Clay, what the hell are you talking about? With your kind of money, what do you do, just pick what you want to do and take over a company?" his friend Mike Masters jokingly said.

"Hell yeah, man!" Clay returned the humor.

They all had a good laugh at the thought. How little did they know the truth that lay behind that statement?

Clay III was from a world neither of them could have ever imagined. A world where his perspective on the future was centered on how much power he could accumulate in a lifetime. Money was simply the tool to amass power.

Both fathers were eager to spend as much time with Montague R. Stanford as they could, and both excitedly agreed to make this a business trip.

Clay had used his unknowing assistant's assistant as a pawn, with the hollow promise of rapid career advancement. His assistant's assistant covertly dealt with Clay III in the strictest of confidence so as not to "upset" his assistant or make him feel that he was being undermined by his subordinate.

"He might feel threatened that your advancement will exceed his," he told the "pawn,"

The pawn's task was to provide a weekend party for several friends with complete discretion, supposedly to protect the wives of his "friends" from their indiscretions. The parties were all-expenses-paid of course, with $10,000 each in cash as spending money. Clay III had already laid the advance ground work by befriending the sons and inviting the fathers to high-profile parties of the Stanford's. An opportunity no politician can refuse.

"This is how the Stanfords party!" he said as he lured them in.

"Nothing like helping little people feel temporarily important." Thinking to himself.

It was an effective tool, developing the skill of manipulating a politician's ego. It allows them to bask in the vast, temporary power they are entrusted with by the public. Their sense of importance becomes so overpowering that they will lose caution and begin to feel entitled to the special treatment. He had done his work well. Clay had selected his political targets prior to picking his financial projects from his father.

He used cutting-edge micro-digital cameras and sound detection devices to outfit the reserved suites at the Palace du Monte Carlo. Each suite reserved for one of his new political "friends."

The political targets were whisked to Monte Carlo via one of the family's three Gulf streams. He then used another low level assistant from one of the family's European companies to secure high-priced college call girls. A task easily accomplished in a city like Paris. They were all irresistibly beautiful, especially to the desperate egos of overweight middle-aged politicians. It worked of course.

No one involved was aware of the other employees or intended outcome.

The trip to Monte Carlo was a success … for Clay anyway.

* * *

Young Clay III, with film in hand of the men scooping up the cash along with the on-camera raunchy "sexcapades," informed the men that they were to ensure the advantage went to his father's bid on the $2 billion dollar state infrastructure projects. Both California State Senators had unblemished political records, and, therefore, their positions were unquestionable.

The deals were sealed and Clay III tasted his first dose of unethical power. And he wanted more.

"The game of power and manipulation is sorta like lawyers dueling in their interpretation of the law. The best brain wins. This addiction is far worse than drugs or alcohol," he warned himself.

This was the same young man, who thought he was the sole heir to his father's fortune, that would later be challenged with sharing an estimated $37.6 billion dollars. That is, unless someone could ensure that the mysterious possible aunt or uncle mentioned in his grandfather's trust stayed out of the picture.

"Power and billion-dollar bank accounts are thicker than any blood I've ever come across." Reminding himself of the ruthlessness and unredeemable dark side of a power addict.

Clay was clear about one thing, he would not be sharing his inherited fortune with anyone, let alone an unknown relative.

"I will do whatever I have to do to protect my rightful position as sole heir." This was a threat and a liability that he could not tolerate. That's how the Stanfords had handled things for generations.

Clay had discreetly involved himself in the discovery of the mythical lost heir since learning of his grandfather's trust provision as a teenager. He had used his own money to maintain a group of investigators outside of his father's law firm. He felt the need to verify the rumors on his own accord. His father had confirmed to him the existence of the trust's provision when asked about it. He also had entrusted his son to do the right thing should it ever become a reality.

Clay III followed the philosopher Seneca, whose favorite motto was, "Luck is when preparation meets opportunity."

* * *

After returning from Monte Carlo, Clay had his assistant contact both politicians and request a meeting at his office at 7:00 p.m. He insisted they attend as it was urgent.

Upon arrival, Congressman Willis was escorted into a large room. A set of heavy red velvet curtains covered the entire wall, which appeared to be a movie screen. He was invited to take a seat in the empty room and told that Mr. Sanford would be with him momentarily. The assistant politely asked if there was "Anything I can get you? A drink perhaps?"

"How about some of the good Scotch he keeps on hand, on the rocks please." Might as well have a taste of that Dalmore 62 while I can, he smiled to himself.

Congressman Willis assumed this was just another surprise from the generous young billionaire. It looked to him like it could be a private screening of a new movie and he half expected others to start arriving at any minute. The congressman sat back and enjoyed his cocktail when the lights started to dim and the curtains slowly began to open, indicating a film was about to be shown. He looked around the room to see if Clay had joined him, but nothing yet. The congressman leaned back in his chair took another sip of his Dalmore 62 and relaxed.

The film opened with a shot of the facade of the Hotel du Paris, the hotel where they had stayed during their trip to Monte Carlo. It then showed the congressman and Senator Masters walking into the lobby of the hotel collecting the keys to their rooms.

Suddenly, there was a loud sound of glass breaking on the tiled floor, as the congressman sat straight up in his chair.

"What the fuck is this! You goddamn dirty son of a bitch!" he yelled at the top of his lungs.

The film now showed the congressman opening and counting the $10,000 dollars that had been waiting for him in his suite provided by his host as spending money.

The scene cut to the action on the bed of the suite with the congressman lying on the bed and a beautiful young French woman demonstrating the local skill of fellatio while he moaned in exhilarating ecstasy. It continued with him turning her over so that he could mount her from behind. Clearly, the film had been made from multiple camera angles.

"Where is that dirty little motherfucker!" he demanded.

"Right here, Congressman," answered Clay, sitting in the back corner of the dark room. He began clapping his hands slowly in applause.

The light in the room began to softly illuminate.

"What a performance, Congressman! Such a race horse for an old coot."

"What do you want, you little prick!" Congressman Willis was so angry he could have murdered Clay right there had he gotten his hands around his throat.

That just wasn't going to happen. Two massive security guards were stationed outside the doors, in full view of the room. More to keep people out than worried about what was going on inside. Besides, as a black belted second Dan in karate Clay Stanford III was hardly worried about a middle-aged politician doing much of anything to him.

"I don't want much, Congressman. Just one little request. It's really nothing compared to the intensity of your impressive screen test."

"Just tell me what the fuck you want, and does it include me getting all the copies of that film?" Now standing while glaring at Clay like a man bent on murder.

"Always willing to please the voter. My kind of politician! Here's the game plan. You see to it that Castle Industries wins the state contract for building all of the high-speed rail passenger stations in California. You do that and we've got ourselves a deal. Make no mistake though, I will destroy your entire life in the span of a few hours if you see take my request any differently than exactly what I have told you to do," Clay stated in a calm, serene voice.

"Done. When and how do I get the film?" the shaking congressman asked in a manner so as not to antagonize Clay.

"Upon the signing of the contracts I will personally deliver the film to you. It is a digital copy and only one was made.

I did the editing myself. Whatcha think? Pretty good, uh? I always thought I could have a career in directing or editing. One thing though, you sure didn't need much directing in that performance!" Giving the congressman a nasty condescending smirk.

"You silly, little, nobody politicians get into office and actually think you are important enough to move around in circles with people like me or my family's level of wealth and power. You are nothing but a paid slave to us. I detest the likes of you. Just remember that if you have any little peasant-brained ideas of double crossing me. Try it by all means, I will relish showing you how the world really works and why we rule the world and the likes of you are only here to serve our needs. When I finish with you will seek the fastest route you can find to suicide. Shits like you always do!

"Now leave before I make you get down on your knees and clean up my floor that you've made a mess of and wasted my $58,000-dollar bottle Scotch. Get out, don't ever contact me again, and keep that vile, silly kid of yours away from me as well!" Clay couldn't believe how powerful he felt. It was the closest thing he had felt to an orgasm outside of an orgasm.

It was now time for the senator's visit.

Senator Master's was seated in the same room as the congressman, who had been there an hour prior. He had become too comfortable around this young man after Monte Carlo. He felt sick in the pit of his stomach at what he had allowed to happen to him there.

"How could I have been so weak and stupid!" he thought with disgust.

"What I did went against everything I've believed in my whole life. What a fool I was to allow myself to get caught up in this outrageous moneyed crowd. I don't belong around those people. Hell, I don't even really like those people. My wife was the one who wanted and pushed for this so-called damned connection. God only knows for what. I hope this is important. I have no more time to waste on this rich kid." Silently exploring his remorse.

"Senator, thank you for coming." Clay snapped him out of his concentration.

"I believe my assistant told you that there was some business that I wanted to discuss with you."

"Yes, Clay, how are you. Nice place you have here."

"Fine, sir, thanks for asking. Let me get right down to business. I know your time is very limited because of your busy schedule. You've been an extraordinary United States Senator for the people of California, sir, one with an almost impeccable record."

Rick Masters did not like how the sound and direction of this conversation made him feel. Monte Carlo was front and center in his mind. His subconscious already knew where this was leading. He prepared himself.

"Yes, I've tried to do what's best for the people of California and my family."

"It's clear that you hold your family in very high esteem."

At this point the heavy velvet red curtains began opening, exposing the large movie screen behind them.

Clay continued talking and showering the senator with praise as the lights dimmed and the film flickered onto the screen.

The filmed commenced right at the point where the senator was reading the note from the envelope of cash. He took the cash out and flipped his thumb over the thick wad of 100 dollar bills, hundreds of them, flipping and folding backwards and forwards. It was a lot of money.

The senator sat quietly. Responding with not even a sigh. Clay had joined the silence as the film rolled.

The senator's naked body popped up on the screen sprawled out on the bed with a beautiful naked redhead licking his chest and him grabbing her face to kiss deeply then rolling on top of her.

"I've seen enough. What do you want?"

"I'm glad you are a straight to the point kind of guy, Senator. I'm running late for a dinner date, and I'd like to wrap this up rather quickly."

"I asked, what is it you want?" Senator Masters coldly asked once again.

"Your assurance that you will see to it that your position on the Federal Transportation Committee fully supports Castle Industries bid for the high-speed rail stations to be built in California.

"And if I don't?" Masters asked, knowing full well what the answer would be.

"Well, let's just say you will experience the end of the world … as you know it."

Senator Rick Masters stood up, buttoned his suit jacket, and stated, "Drop dead, you slimy, little piece of shit" then walked out of the room without so much as a glance in Clay's direction.

"That one's going to be a problem," Clay smirked to himself.

Clay would deny any involvement except to have invited the senator and his son, as family friends, to a weekend event. One of the many they had attended since meeting at his parents well-known annual Emerald Ball earlier that year. His father was clearly not associated with the senator as he had only met him once that evening at the ball. The senator would have to implicate the congressman, who would deny it all, in order to conjure up any sort of worthy lie. That was highly unlikely.

Clay could not be touched; he was sure of it. He had made it so that any two people in the planning of the scheme did not know each other or his involvement in his scheme.

Chapter Twenty-Nine

EVERYBODY FINDS OUT

Walking back to his car, shaking and sweating with anxiety, Rocco jumped into his car, sat, and stared into blank space. He took a deep breath and exhaled slowly.

"Who killed you, Dotty?" Was all he could muster. After what seemed like fifteen minutes, he picked up his cell phone and dialed Elsa.

"Listen, we've got to meet right now. Drop whatever you are doing and meet me at Schwab's."

"I can't, I'm in the middle of tracking a wire transfer that went into Dotty's account."

"Trust me, what I have to tell you will be the most unbelievable thing you have ever heard in your life. Now get your ass over there pronto!" He was still in a state of shock as he drove to Schwab's. Rocco debated for a second if it would be best to share this information with Elsa outside of Schwab's, considering all that was going on.

"Maybe I should tell her inside the police car, just in case." His thoughts moved to Dotty's daughter, young Brit. How would he tell her? Surely this should benefit her in some way. "Is it possible that the Stanfords could be involved in her murder? Does the senior Stanford know about his lost sister?"

When Elsa arrived, he motioned for her to join him in his parked police car. Elsa jumped into the car and turned to Rocco.

"What's so important that I couldn't finish finding out who dropped 30 grand into Dotty's account?"

"What I have to tell you is going to take this murder investigation where no murder investigation in Hollywood has ever gone before," Rocco stoically told Elsa.

"Well, what is it? You look like you've just pissed in your pants or seen a ghost!"

"Dotty Henderson was … IS, the biological daughter of Clay and Gemma Stanford II!"

"Holy, Jesus, mighty God!"

"Confirmed!"

Elsa was speechless.

"I just spent the afternoon with a woman Dotty knew as her aunt. The old woman was in reality the midwife, black market baby provider extraordinaire, the one who delivered her, then handled her adoption. Secretly, for none other than Gemma Huntington Stanford. I've seen the documents that prove it."

"But why did Gemma give the baby up?"

"That the old lady wasn't sure of. She suspected it was because of an affair with another man. Her black chauffeur. Only, the baby was not his, obviously. It was her husband's, Clay."

"This is big, Rocco! I mean really big! We've got to figure out how to handle this. We gotta move fast before someone else gets a hold of this."

"Don't I know it, partner."

"By the way, that shit, Jacques, sold his story about the fight between Vivien and Dotty to the rags!"

"Ya know, he's still very much on my short list of suspects. Maybe you ought to give him some advice about keeping that fat trap of his shut before he moves up a few more notches. I mean it, Els!"

"On it. Shall we powwow with the captain tonight? He'll want a press conference tomorrow. How do we handle the Stanfords and the news?"

* * *

Detective Rocco Goldman was nervous. He knew that he had stumbled onto something that was about to change his life and career forever. He just needed to make sure he did it right. Every step he made from this point on would be scrutinized in detail. He also knew this was going to scare the shit out of his captain.

He and Elsa had been up all night reviewing evidence, motives, and suspects. What they were about to present to the captain could either blow the case wide open or cost him a promotion.

"So, what the hell do you have to tell me amidst this goddamn soap opera of a murder that is such an emergency? I hope to hell it is worth calling me away from those peoples" homes that are sliding down the Hollywood Hills in this rain."

"I believe it is. In fact, sir, this is just not to be believed."

"Who's your suspect? The husband, boyfriend, a goddamn movie star?"

"Clay Stanford III!"

"Are you fucking out of your mind! This better be good, 'cause it is not what I wanted to hear."

"I know, Captain, but let me explain. I didn't want to believe it either. For Christ sake, the Stanfords are the last people on earth I would want to fuck with. This is what we have."

Rocco proceeded to tell his story about the old lady, while backing it with a subpoena if needed. With that he slapped the file down on the captain's desk and gave him a step by step run down.

"We think Clay may have found out that Dotty was related and might have some kind of claim to that enormous fortune, of which he just happens to be sole heir." He told the captain about how the stranger at Schwab's turned out to be a PI/lawyer hired by Clay III. The old lady confirmed that the PI had paid her a visit as well. "We believe he may have killed her because of her true identity. We don't believe Dotty had a clue about any of it. If she had, she wouldn't have been stealing and selling gossip to the tabloids." Rocco finished his hard sell to the captain.

"There's a lot we can learn from Mr. Clay III. Looking on the bright side, he might be able to clear this up. I'll make the call to Mr. Stanford," the captain replied.

Rocco was relieved. The captain seemed to have agreed with his assessment.

"Mr. Stanford, very sorry to bother you. We would not have disturbed you and your family had your son not hired the private investigator seeking information on Mrs. Henderson."

"Well, Captain, I have no issues with your detectives asking my son a few questions. I may, however, be able to help in clearing up some of it. You see, my father's estate carries with it a stipulation that requires his descendants to maintain an ongoing search for a mythical sibling of mine that no one has ever proven even existed. I won't bore you with the private details of why they supposedly went missing. It was a very long time ago, and my father could be rather eccentric at times. In fact, I have had my own private investigator from time to time, even outside of the estates requirements. You might say, it's the occasional sentimentally of losing my family when I was young. Normally, the executor of the estate handles it. This is important for a number of reasons. If there is a sister of mine in existence, and she or her heirs are ever located, she or they would be entitled to half of my estate. Or, should I say, my parents' estate. I'm not sure why Clay zeroed in on Mrs.—what was her name again?"

"Mrs. Henderson," the captain answered.

"Yes … Mrs. Henderson. I hadn't been informed of any possible connection to her. Frankly, she sounds as if she would be the least likely person to end up as a lost Stanford. We never know though, do we, Captain? I trust that our conversation is strictly confidential."

"Yes, of course, Mr. Stanford," the captain obliged.

"As for the other questions, you will have to address those with my son Clay. I'm sure he has a perfectly valid reason for doing what he did."

Clay thought the police might come knocking on his door. Particularly after his PI was strong armed by the police into giving up his mission details. He was right.

His father informed him of the call and that he had had four family lawyers present for the lengthy conversation with the Hollywood Police Captain. The call included information about his father's trust regarding a potentially lost family member. Montague was perplexed.

"Has Clay found something out and not shared it with me? But why?" Montague didn't know whether to be disturbed, excited, or worried.

The captain rang Rocco on his cell. He and Elsa were on their way to revisit Jacques and Vivien when they pulled over to take the call. It's a good thing they had.

"Just spoke to Mr. Stanford Sr., The father. He has no qualms about you speaking to his son, as long as he is accompanied by his lawyers that is. Notice I used plural. We had quite the conversation. He informed me of something that will definitely throw some gasoline on your fire. Apparently, he has a missing sister, or an unknown sister. A child that is referenced in his father's estate. A codicil that ensures half of everything goes to this sister or brother should they ever be found." The Captain stated.

"Wow! That's sounds like quite the motive. Had he been able to confirm Dotty's DNA he would have learned that she was the lost sister. Based on the family trust set up by the grandfather, Dotty was heir to billions. If Dotty is out of the way, I guess it all reverts back to Clay III."

"Bingo … my boy!"

"Cap, this is just fucking incredible!" Rocco excitedly blurted out.

"Watch your fucking language when speaking to your superior, boy!"

"Yes sir." They both had a little chuckle to relieve the unbelievable stress of the case.

"The clincher will be, did Clay III know that Dotty had been verified through her DNA as the missing heir?"

Rocco looked towards Elsa, who was trying to make out what the captain was saying by leaning over the cell phone near Rocco's ear."

He ended the call, then turned to Elsa.

"Dotty Henderson, tabloid hustling waitress from Schwab's, was a goddamn heiress to a billion-dollar fortune and never knew it! Now if that is not jaw dropping!"

Elsa and Rocco had to find out if there was any connection between Clay and Dotty's murder.

"In the meantime, I'm going to take a little trip to Palm Springs to meet Mr. Max Moriel, the actor," Rocco told Elsa.

The drive through the desert allowed him to go over and debate all the angles and evidence he had accumulated so far. The subpoena of some of Dotty's tabloid clients had helped with the number of potential suspects. Max Moriel had been one of them. "I guess Dotty was responsible for a lot of PR damage," He thought about all of Dotty's secrets that began to unfold during the investigation.

Upon arriving at his home, it was clear to Rocco that the former leading man had fallen on hard times from the look of the run-down, weather-beaten small cottage he now called home. The cottage was protected by a broken picket fence with peeling light gray paint that had started out as white.

"Thanks for meeting with me, Mr. Moriel."

"Max, please."

Rocco noticed the large bandage on Max's right hand as he sat across from him. When Max saw him looking, he eased the injured had down to his side and out of sight.

"So, you used to know the victim?"

"Not well, I was a regular customer of her at Schwab's for a while. My studio was just a few blocks from Sunset and Vine, and I liked the atmosphere. Can't say I knew much about the waitress, Dotty."

"Do you get up to Hollywood very often these days?"

"Not if I can help it."

"Hollywood left you with a bad taste did it?"

"To say the least."

"I'm aware of what happened, Mr. Moriel. The leak to the tabloids about your private life. My question is, did you ever find out who divulged this information?"

"No, not that it would make any difference. Can I get you a coffee, detective?"

"Yes, that would be great, cream and one sugar. What do you mean?"

"I've read the papers about that horrible woman. I hardly think I was the only famous person she ratted out. Sounds to me there is an army of people who had good reason to permanently shut her trap. I wasn't one of them."

"Where were you in Hollywood on the date of the murder?" Rocco asked as he snatched a used band aid from the table with a baggie while the actor's back was turned fixing coffee.

"No, I was here."

"Alone?"

"Yes, I'm always alone these days."

"Well, sir, thank you for your time. I will be in touch."

"I'll get a forensic test on the to see if we have a match with the killer's blood," thought the detective.

* * *

Brit had just finished rereading the current *MOUTH* magazine, which carried a picture of her father and his young girlfriend splashed across the front page headline, "$$$$WAS it for the money! … Secret girlfriend denies involvement in murder, hacked into victim's email account!"

Brit was in tears, alone, grief stricken over the loss of her mother, and now this. She was having to constantly face the barrage of daily tabloid trash that made her life a living hell.

"I want to just leave here and never come back!" she said to herself through streaming tears.

"I just need to make it through this last class for graduation."

She heard the keys in the door and rushed downstairs to confront her father.

"How could you do that to us! Mother loved you! She was devoted to you! I hate your guts!" was what stumbled out of her hysterical and sobbing mouth.

Ralph pleaded with her. He tried to tell her that it was the young woman that had pursued him, and that he loved his wife dearly.

"I am just as heartbroken," he told her while sobbing just as much.

Poor Brit, she was yet to find out that her loving mother had been the first to betray her and Ralph. A betrayal that had started over 10 years ago.

"Everything seems like its crumbling around me. How could everything be so normal and wonderful one day and completely destroyed the next? This is by far the darkest hour of my life. I don't know if I can handle anymore," she sobbed into her pillow.

Sadly, she didn't have long to wait to find out what was coming next. Brit woke the next morning to see the headlines of the *National Radar*, "Love Triangle at the HEART of Hollywood murder! … The boss, the waitress, and the vixen fiancée." The story went into great detail about Dotty's long-term affair of the flesh with her boss, Sam O'Brien.

The story was offering up it's own theory that it may have been the boss's fiancée who offed the sex-driven snooping waitress.

"*National Radar*'s sources are reporting that police have a witness to a heated and threatening fight that occurred between the victim, her ex-SEX partner, and his violent fiancée. It is being reported that the fiancée allegedly threaten to send her to the grave if she didn't leave her future husband alone!"

The source turned out to be none other than Jacques. He figured out a way to extract his revenge on Dotty and make some cash the old Dotty way, sell his story to the tabloids. He'd pocketed a cool $12,000 for the inside information.

* * *

Michael Deeves gave the Tripartite his usual devilish smile as he stopped by their table to say hello.

"Good morning, Bombshells!"

"Hey there, handsome!" they greeted him in unison, all smiling as usual whenever Michael stopped by.

He leaned in and gave them all kisses on the cheeks.

"May I speak to you lovely ladies for a sec?"

"Sure."

"We are all aware of what's gone down with Dotty, right?"

"Honey, you couldn't help from knowing unless you've been buried under a rock." Indignant, Irene shared her quip with an air of dismissal.

"Lord, yes," piped in Maria-Angela, while Natasha just shook her head up and down several times.

"Well, remember her sweet little girl Brit?" The ladies became somewhat silent. Their indignant facial expressions softening into that of concern and sympathy.

"How is she?" Irene asked, as the other two keenly waited for the answer.

"Not well as you can imagine. Regardless of what we think of Dotty, and believe me, you don't know the half of it, there is an innocent, sweet young woman out there pretty much alone right now.

"I remember her well, so adorable," Natasha offered.

"I'm taking donations to help her get through this nightmare. I've asked her to meet me for lunch today."

The three women immediately opened up their purses and pooled $153 dollars and handed it to Michael.

"Hold on a minute, Michael" Irene pulled out her checkbook and wrote out an additional check for $200 dollars.

"I remembered that she is in school and the market has been good to me lately."

"Thank you so much, ladies. Dotty had a dark side, but we must not forget the good, and Brit had no part in this. You all are wonderful people. All of you, thank you." The three of them pulled him in for another hug and kiss. A $500 dollar donation from Cino and Victoria adding it to $3000 given from Chalon, Gavin, Summer, and Sam. The only unwilling member of the Schwab's group of regulars who did not give was Jacques, who refused to give a nickel.

Michael knew Dotty a bit better than the others and she had always shown a genuine interest in his work over the years as he wrote and drank her coffee for hours on end.

"I'll offer to take Brit under my wing if I have to. I'm pretty sure I remember Dotty and Ralph not having very much family here. If she's left alone, those fucking tabloids will eat her alive." Thinking to himself while getting protective.

Brit was unbearably depressed.

"How could everything be normal and happy one day, then you wake and your entire world has been turned upside down, inside out!" she confided in a friend.

Every night before falling asleep she wondered to herself, "Who am I, and who is my mother's other family?"

Her father's family lived in the East and there was only a few of them.

"Considering what has happened, Aunt Marjorie has got to tell me whatever it is she knows about my mother. I want to see those documents. If only to save what little sanity I have left. I just can not go through life in this state." Fighting back an endless reservoir of tears. The crying would just erupt morning, noon, and night.

She jumped at the ringing phone. She was startled as it pierced the silent thought she was engulfed in and picked it up out of reflex, hesitating, thinking it might be one of those awful papers. She mustered a forceful, "Hello!"

"Brit?"

"Who is this?" Thinking that she recognized the voice, then instantly doubting herself. Immediately convinced it was just a sense of desperation of wanting to recognize it.

"It's Michael Deeves, a friend of your mother's, remember me?"

"Oh Michael! It is so nice to hear from you!" Sounding more like a plea than a hello.

"How are you holding up?"

"Not well. I kinda don't know which way to turn right now. I'm sure you've read all the horrible things those papers are saying. On top of my mom's … ." She couldn't bring herself to say the word.

"I called to see if you are available for lunch today?"

"Yes, yes, yes. I would love that!"

"Don't worry about a thing. I've been a little worried about you. I'll pick you up at 11:00, is that OK?"

"That sounds great!"

"What's the new address in Sherman Oaks?"

"Thank you, Michael."

Brit was very thankful that Michael had called. It helped she couldn't just hide from the world and that she needed to pull her life back together. And more importantly, that she wasn't all alone in the world even with the fight going on between her and her father.

Chapter Thirty

THE RISE OF BRIT!

"Wow! Look at you! It seems like you were just starting college yesterday. Now, you are so grown up!"

"And on my own now," she spoke sadly.

Michael gave her a big tight hug.

"You've got your father and you will always have us. Listen, I know it hasn't been easy with all that trash printed in those terrible rags, but understand that you can depend on some of us. We've known your mother for a very long time. I saw her everyday."

"They all hate her now."

"That's not true, not at all. We really don't know what she did and did not do. What your mother did might appear to have been underhanded, but don't lose sight of the fact that in many respects that's how business and success is conducted in this town. And we might not like it, but that's the reality of it."

"I am so confused by it all, Michael. Her cheating on Dad. And Dad cheating on her."

"That part is a little out of my league. I'm afraid I wasn't privy to those actions. I knew your mother as a decent person. More importantly, her actions do not have to be the light that guides you in life. We all must make our own path in the world, Brit."

"If only I had some family to turn to."

"Life is about mountains and valleys, you can not appreciate the mountains without experiencing the valleys. And I believe you have a ton of beautiful mountains in your future. You will be a stronger person down the road after all of this blows over."

"I hope so. Though, I can't imagine that right now. I just want to tide you over for a little while. We know you just finished school, so it's kinds of a graduation present from us."

With that Michael handed Brit an envelope full of cash and checks.

She was speechless. "I don't know how to thank you. Thank you from the bottom of my heart. I wasn't even sure if I was going to be able to stay with my father considering what happened."

"It's the least we could do for you." Michael hugged her again.

"Please let the others know how grateful I am. I'd come by to thank them personally, but I don't think that I can ever go inside Schwab's again, which is strange because I have so many happy memories growing up there." Sounding very melancholy.

The next day, Brit was left a note by her father telling her that he had been informed that Dotty had left a will. He had a copy of it for her.

"P.S. Your mother left bank accounts totaling $1.1 million dollars, plus this paid for, clear-titled house we just moved into. Don't ask me how, I have no idea. I miss you, Love Daddy."

"Where on earth did Mama get that kind of money? The tabloids? Could she have possibly made that much money?" These were questions that she most likely would never find the answers to.

The will explained how "my current possessions, including cash, is to be shared equally between my only child, Brit, and my beloved husband Ralph."

"She had loved Daddy after all. He still doesn't deserve a penny after cheating on her. Then she wondered if he had found out about her cheating?" She was afraid to ask.

"I have to talk to him. I really need some kind of closure, especially with this hurricane swirling around me."

"I just want to know who I am, and who did my mother come from. If I can only figure out my next step in life. Just little things like everyone else." She managed a light smile.

"Aunt Marjorie, it's Brit. I need to see you."

"Come on over, dear. I'd love to see you too."

Brit threw a disguise on and fled out the side entrance of the house and walked down the alley to her car parked on a street around the corner.

"Finally, I am going to get some straight answers out of Aunt Marjorie!" She was determined not to leave until she had the answers once and for all.

"Aunt Marjorie, I know mother was adopted. What do you know about this and I really want to see those papers? Now!"

The feeble old lady told her everything as she read every document in her aunt's possession. It was too unbelievable to comprehend.

"And that's why I never told your mother," the old lady said.

The information from her aunt … or the old lady whom she always assumed was her aunt, just about sent her over the edge. She sat numb, with a blank stare on her face until her old aunt started crying.

"You are going to hate me now. I know it. Honey, I've loved you and your mother as if you were my own. I was even going to take your mother and raise her had George not come along around the same time. Then your Uncle John died suddenly right after George's birth. Please don't hate me."

"I could never hate you, Auntie. So, you are telling me mother never knew any of this all through the years? She never had any idea that she came from one of the wealthiest families in the world? Didn't you ever try to tell her about her real mother?"

"I couldn't because I had given my word. Later on, after I had a change of heart, there was just no way to contact her mother because, unfortunately, they had all perished in that awful sinking of the *Andrea Doria* in '56. Also, they could have destroyed me or had me put in jail, and I had a baby to raise. Oh, please, my dear, try to understand," Brit's aunt pleaded with her while sobbing.

"I do. I want you to know, I love you more than I ever have. You have lifted a very heavy burden from my soul," Brit assured her.

"Thank you, my little one. Thank you for understanding." Her old aunt was grateful.

"My mother was always impressed by people who seemed to have more material possessions than us. She struggled so hard to give me things she never had. And that passion of hers to live in Sherman Oaks! It used to drive me nuts! How odd it is to find out that she came from a family that could buy half of Los Angeles."

"What are you going to do, dear?"

"Does anyone else know about this?" she asked.

"Only the police. They came here wanting to know about your mother's history. They seemed to know that I was a relative. Well ... you know what I mean."

"Yes, auntie. I am the one who told them about you. I mean that you were a relative of ours. Does any of the Stanford family know?" Brit nervously asked

"That I don't know. Just be careful, my sweet one. Rich, powerful families can be dangerous people sometimes when their money is involved. I want you to promise me you will take care of yourself," the aunt begged.

"I will, aunt Marjorie, I give you my word."

Saying goodbye to her aged aunt, Brit held her tighter than she had ever held her before, holding on to her as if she were a direct link to her mother. This was the same woman that had helped bring her mother into the world as a baby. She couldn't imagine feeling any closer to an aunt.

"Now, I have to figure out what to do with all of this. Do I try to make contact with them? They will probably think I am some crazy nut job. Maybe I should talk to detective Rocco and Elsa about what to do. I'll wait before telling Dad any of this." Finally, a small amount of calm had returned to his state of being.

She had started down the path to find out who she was. Half of her was a Stanford.

"Now, I only hope that Dad is a real Henderson at this point." She managed a smile and a light giggle.

One thing she did not intend to let happen was for those filthy tabloids to get a hold of this. "They'll destroy what little shred of a possible future I still have."

"Can you imagine, 'Lost billionaire heiress turned waitress with tawdry past.' No thank you, very much!"

"I wonder if I am even legally one of them, a Stanford?" Maybe Michael can help?" she thought.

Chapter Thirty-One

BATTLE WITH CLAY

THE CONGRESSMAN WAS ABIDING BY HIS BLACKMAIL AGREEMENT with Clay III. He saw to it that the initial vote for Castle's bid was approved.

The senator was a different story. He refused and did all he could to see to that Castle Industries was not chosen. He also knew that his entire life was about to implode before him. Could he fight back? He debated with himself as to what his options where. Even if he exposed Clay with accusations, he had no proof.

Senator Masters had worked hard for everything he held dear in life, his family, profession, beliefs, honor. Yet, he had allowed it all to slip away with the temptation of overpowering wealth and decadence.

He spent many nights alone wondering what had motivated him to go on that fateful trip to Monte Carlo, without his wife or son. Why had he thrown all caution to the wind with such a reckless abandonment?

"As much as I despise that piece of shit Clay Stanford III, I have no one to blame but myself," he owned it.

It was him and him alone that had to face the consequences.

He spent that evening in the pews of the massive cathedral of St. Thomas. A huge church that could probably seat a few thousand worshipers. There were just a few other worshipers present, all lost in prayer or meditation.

Rick Masters walked through the huge doors drenched from the pouring rain. He was thankful that the silent emptiness of the vast church welcomed him as just another lost soul.

"I look around at those other two believers kneeling in prayer, positive that neither of them are facing the end of life as I am." He didn't say this out of self pity. He stated it as a simple fact. He knew his wife would divorce him, his son would hate him, he would cast a stain upon his family, and lose the trust of the people he served. He was no longer worthy of any of it. Whatever the outcome, he was far from the precipice of suicide. That would have to wait … at least until he had extracted his searing revenge. It was at that moment he made up his mind to face the coming storm that was about to shatter his life.

"I will tell my wife first and foremost."

His fall would be swift and steep, that much he was certain of. He had tried to do the right thing throughout his life. He'd led an exemplary life up until that moment.

"How could I have allowed a kid of 24 to manipulate me in such an easy manner? Why would it matter that he did it to blackmail me? He's worth billions, they would never believe that he needed a crooked deal."

He couldn't prove anything. Clay Stanford had been terribly generous to him and his son. Besides, the construction company belonged to his father. There simply was nothing to link Clay to the blackmail. He bowed, leaned forward, put his head in his clasped hands, and prayed.

"I pray for your forgiveness, Heavenly Father."

Thirty minutes later, rising from his knees, he had but one thought burning in his mind. "No friend ever served me, and no enemy ever wronged me, whom I have not repaid in full."

So stated his historical mentor, General Lucius Corniallius Sulla. Now he was determined to seek his revenge.

"I will seek it silently, methodically, and patiently, but I shall have it before I leave this world" was his spiritual conclusion as a man facing total destruction of all he knew and loved. He was now at peace and accepted in his heart the inevitable.

Clay III wasted no time in unleashing his devastating attack on the senator. By the next morning anonymous packages arrived with no return address to *MOUTH*, *National Radar*, Mrs. Masters, The U.S. Senate's Majority Leader, and the Senate's Select Committee on Ethics. The packages contained copies of the film starring Senator Masters shot on location in Monte Carlo.

The retribution was immediate and shattering. Senator Masters was stripped of all committee posts effective immediately. His resignation was requested by the President via the Vice President as head of the U.S. Senate.

Within a week's time he was censured by the Senate, which promptly launched an investigation.

His wife ordered him out of their home, and he was excommunicated by his son. Rick Masters found that he was generally persona non grata wherever he went.

The tabloids had renamed him "The Seedy, Stealing, Sex-crazed Senator from Monte Carlo."

He hid out by the beach in a cheap $65.00 dollar a night motel.

Mrs. Masters filed for divorce the same week, and proceeded to set his boxed belongings in the garage for him to pick up.

"He's dead as far as I'm concerned" was her only statement to the press.

His son hung up on him after telling him, "Don't ever contact me again."

No one from his past would have anything to do with him except his elderly mother. His father refused to even acknowledge him on the phone when he called, passing it to his mother without a word.

Senator Masters responded with his resignation from the Senate and agreed to the divorce, giving his wife whatever she wanted. He also respected his son's wishes and never attempted to contact him again.

He fell from a personal net worth of $4 million dollars to $150,000 left to him by his wife.

Then he disappeared from the face of the earth.

"It has all come to pass and I am still alive. Alive only because I will have my revenge."

Occasionally, he walked along the beach and the marina, instinctively holding his head down when passing others out of fear of being recognized, afraid that if they stared those few extra seconds he would be discovered. He was desperately lonely as he would replay his former life over and over in his head, aimlessly staring at the beautiful yachts anchored in the evening light. He unknowingly strolled past the gigantic yacht *Cosmos* when he recognized Clay III amongst the people on board. While standing a safe distance away, he watched as the cocktail party onboard unfolded and the sun sank into the sea. He recalled how Clay had informed him that he spent all of his weekends onboard the family's yacht, and how much he loved the sea because it provided him with all of his favorite foods. That he was in fact a huge lover of almost all seafood. The details came flooding back as he inhaled the fresh ocean air. The smell of the sea and salt water refreshed him. He remembered Clay had introduced them to his sushi chef one weekend as they enjoyed a ride out to Avalon onboard the yacht.

"That's it! I've found the crack in his armor!" he quietly told himself.

With that, his face filled with color again and the air invigorated him. He couldn't sleep that night as his mind raced from thought to thought.

"I'll enroll in a sushi academy tomorrow."

"The marina will be the perfect place for me to rebuild my life." He had found the light that was to guide him out of darkness.

The ex-senator threw himself into his new mission. He located and enrolled in a condensed professional sushi master class. He was an excellent, determined student driven by his revenge. He spent his down time learning every detail he could about the life of Clay III. From a safe distance he learned all he could about the weekend comings and goings aboard the *Cosmos*.

It was a massive, beautiful yacht with a large staff to run her. It appeared that Clay III was the primary user of it on a regular basis.

Masters kept up with Clay III's successful bid in securing the state construction contract, spearheaded by the congressman who also received a hefty re-election donation from him.

The *Cosmos* sat unused during the week, except for the permanent staff aboard. Rick took advantage of this time to strike up friendships with members of the crew. He introduced himself as a fellow yacht owner and marina neighbor. During these casual conversations, he learned who the master chef was and waited for the day to begin an unassuming conversation on the docks with the chef regarding food. This in turn led Rick to extend an invitation to the chef for a chat on the boat.

"Its really a pretty sweet job because it's only the son that spends very much time onboard, and he is a seafood and raw vegetables kind of guy," the chef shared.

"Wow! I'm a seafood fanatic myself. What does he prefer?" Rick casually asked.

This led to the discussion of Clay's passion for seafood delicacies.

"Sashimi, lots of shellfish, mussels, clams, and when I can get it, blowfish! His favorite is fugu, I'm a licensed fugu chef. Been with the family for four years. Terrific people, very kind and generous. You'd think the young man would be a spoiled brat, him being the sole heir to all those billions! Not at all! We love him!" The chef seemed willing to keep talking, so Rick let him.

"Its amazing what a few bottles of pinot grigio aboard a beautiful rented yacht can do," The ex-senator thought, smiling to himself at the success of his undercover accomplishment.

Rick overheard from his covert observations that both chef Kazuo and his employer, Clay Stanford, were great connoisseurs of Italian opera.

"I hope you don't mind the Verdi and Puccini," Rick said to the chef.

"Are you joking! I am in heaven, man! Outside of my love for food and wine, opera is my passion!" the chef told him.

"You are a class act, Chef Kazuo."

"You know, Jason, I'd like to introduce you to Mr. Stanford this weekend. I've only extended this kind of invitation a few times in all these years, but I think the two of you would get along great." Referring to Rick's alias.

"That's a terrific show of friendship, Kazuo. Unfortunately, I'll be away this weekend, maybe some other time," he lied as coolly as an Oscar winning leading man.

"Some other time then."

"Not if I can help it, my friend," Rick thought to himself. "By the way, who's your seafood supplier? I am always on the lookout for the best."

"Man oh man, do I have one for you! He's very expensive, but the best in L.A. Always the freshest you can find. I've used him for the last two years. Comes from a family that's been in the fishing business for 70 years. His name is Kai Miyako, I can give you his number," the chef volunteered.

"That would be great! And I'll owe you some fresh sashimi!" replied Rick

"This sure is a beautiful boat you have, man!" admired Chef Kazuo.

"It's for sale! Wanna buy it?" They laughed and toasted with another glass of pinot in the Villeroy & Boch crystal.

* * *

Rick showed up on the fishing docks in Malibu to meet the seafood supplier the next day. He told the fisherman that he was in training and was looking for a five-star quality supplier, then slipped him a crisp, new $100-dollar bill. He was in.

The fisherman quickly cozied up to him after Rick slipped him $100 extra when he alerted him that he was selling the top stuff to him first. Rick stroked his ego, "Hey, Kai, I'm finishing up master sushi chef training and I'd like to maybe get some feedback from some top clients if I could. I have an offer for you that's a win win for both of us. Let me prepare some beautiful, first class sashimi platters for a few of your clients and you can submit them as yours in appreciation for their business. All I ask for in return is their feedback. You can let me know what they think? It's as easy as that! You get the praise; I get the feedback. I hear you have some of the Top Dogs!" As he slipped him another $100.

"Not some, but the top! How about the Stanford family! Been supplying them for a couple years now, both for their yacht and in town … exclusively!" he proudly boasted.

"Wow! That is impressive, man! Well then, I'll make it especially for the Stanfords!"

"You know what, Jason, you've got yourself a deal!" Kai said while thinking what a score he was getting out of this.

"I'll make sure you get my first big order and all the ones after that!" He'd sealed the deal.

* * *

"Showtime!" Rick smiled to himself. "This will be a meal that little motherfucker will never forget. In fact, hopefully, it will be his last memory on earth."

Rich Masters, ex U.S. Senator, newly licensed sushi chef, and man with a vendetta spent the evening meticulously preparing the food. Every detail was adhered to.

He played "The Flower Duet" by Viens, between Lakme and Mallika in Leo Delibes' opera *Lakme* while he prepared his nemesis' last supper. The opera's magnificent melody melded perfectly as he slowly sliced through the delicate flesh of the deadly seafood. The food that would free him from what had become the unearthly bonds of his torturer and master … revenge.

"No. There will be no suicide for me, not yet anyway."

He rose early that Saturday morning after the deepest sleep he had experienced since before Monte Carlo. For the first time since his fall into the depths of despair, he smiled at himself in the mirror. He did not allow judgment to enter into the final steps of his perceived freedom from this disgraced hell. It was time for the star of this unfortunate drama to be served for the last time.

He met Kai on the pier.

"Morning, Jason!" Sam enthusiastically greeted the ex-senator by his alias.

I've prepared something very special for Mr. Stanford, and I brought a sample for you to try as well. I only ask that you make sure you deliver it as is. Unwrapped, it risks the danger of losing its freshness and I've sealed it so that it can only be opened once. Trust me, you will definitely be hearing from them after he tastes this! I've gone a little overboard to impress them."

"Thank you, my friend! I think this will work out for both of us! Just don't forget who helped you get your start! These platters look incredible!" He couldn't believe his luck.

"Jason, I will never forget what you've done for me. Never." He had never spoken truer words.

* * *

Clay III had two major loose ends to wrap up. The senator and Dotty, aka "that atrocious woman" as he referred to his newly discovered aunt.

He later tried to explain his actions of hiring a private investigator to his father.

"I did it as a surprise for you, Dad. Imagine, what a gift it would be for you, if in fact it turned out to be true, and I found her on my own accord without you knowing it! Sadly, Pop, she wasn't the one. Thank goodness, considering what just happened." Referring to Dotty's murder.

What he did not tell his father was that he was the one! Dotty was his father's long-lost sister and the missing child of Clay Stanford II. She was without a doubt real, but she was now dead. A victim of a heinous murder.

"Then, there's that ex-senator … what's his name? I wonder how he's enjoying his new found fame as a X-rated film star!" Emphasizing the letter X as he turned to face the floor to ceiling window in his office. The expansive view of Los Angeles at his feet, a metaphor for his life at the top.

"I did a pretty good job if I may say so myself. There was no way in hell I was about to allow that atrocious, cheap waitress to come out of nowhere and collect half of what is mine by birth! Selling dirt to the tabloids for a living. How on earth could that low-life woman possibly carry the same bloodline as my father! That test may have confirmed it, but I will never accept it. Good luck in solving that murder!" He let out a low snicker to himself. He was the sole heir and he intended to keep it that way.

Clay had discovered that Dotty had been the source for the devastating leak regarding actor Max Moriel. His career had come to a screeching halt after the tabloids published pictures of him "dolled up in his female attire."

Clay secretly sought him out. He'd been located living in a small run-down house on the outskirts of Palm Springs.

The place was hardly a reflection of the past grandeur Max Moriel had known in his Hancock Park estate; sold off to satisfy creditors when the income vanished. The Palm Springs house was located on the edge of a strip mall, with a front yard framed by a small, broken, peeling white fence that was turning gray from the blowing dirt in the harsh desert summers and also had a few missing planks. Tumbleweeds in the front yard were the only sign of vegetation on the barren ground that had been reclaimed by the desert.

He was promptly informed of who and how his private life was turned over to the worst of the worst tabloid, *MOUTH!*. Max was stunned to learn it had been Dotty who ratted on him and cost him his career. He had been extremely generous to Dotty, the waitress at Schwab's in Hollywood, every time he'd eaten there. Tipping her with $20 to $50 dollars regardless of how small his bill had been.

Moreover, he wasn't quite sure who this man was or why he was offering this information to him, but he was grateful.

"I'm just a dedicated fan. I thought it was horrifying what happened to you, and I thought you should know who did it. Your fans, including me, were very upset!" was the line given by Clay.

Max had been sold the story that Dotty had done this to lots of people.

"I'm listening. As you can see, I haven't much left in life after that story ran. No career, no one would hire me. No lover, no one could tolerate my state of depression. No money, my crooked manager had consumed most of that, along with creditors feasting on the rest." All he had left were his memories.

"Sometimes I wonder why I even get up in the morning." Spoken from the mouth of a broken man.

"I almost wished I liked alcohol or drugs. Just to be able to numb the pain. I think about how sad it is that it all went away simply because of who I loved. My poor girlfriend Angelica was too young to deal with the impact of having her face in those pictures. It destroyed her."

"You mean the young lady that committed suicide?" Clay asked.

"Yes."

"Mr. Moriel, I can offer you this, enclosed in this envelope is enough money for you to use for whatever you like or you can use to strike back against the person who stole your life from you. Just know that you were not the first one whose life was destroyed by this terrible woman, and most likely not the last. One can only hope that someone puts a stop to that one-woman wrecking ball before more lives like Angelica's are taken. It's not as if anyone would miss her. I doubt if her own family would miss someone so awful." Encouraging the lost star to take things into his own hands.

"What do I have to lose," Max said. He was beginning to like the idea that was subtly being presented to him.

He answered his own questioned. "Absolutely nothing."

It wasn't long before he received a call from the detective investigating Dotty's murder, Detective Rocco Goldman. Shortly after the detective's visit, Max Moriel was arrested as he tried to board a flight to Switzerland. They discovered $5,000 dollars in cash on him. Moriel's blood matched the blood at Dotty's crime scene. He was held as a prime suspect. He told the police he was visited by a man claiming to be a fan who informed him about that Dotty had been behind his leaked private pictures.

"That's him. That's the man that visited me and gave me the money as a gift from my fans. That's what he said to me. I thought about vengeance, but decided to let it go, move to Europe and start fresh." Max identified Clay III from a photograph.

* * *

Montague wasted no time in launching his own investigation after being informed by the captain as to Clay being sought as a suspect.

"Mr. Sanford, we have some information for you," the two men dressed in identical black suits told him as they met in his office.

The look of concern was obvious. He determined that it was one of two things. They had found his lost sibling or Clay was in serious trouble.

It was both.

"What have you got?" he asked with a seriousness that reflected his interpretation of the men's body language.

With that, one of the two men gently laid a file down on Montague's desk. "It's all in there, sir."

"Is Clay in trouble?" Montague asked.

"Not that we can tell, so far. There are some unanswered questions as to what he knows about your other question, sir."

"You mean my missing sibling?"

"Yes, your sister, sir."

"Dear God! It's true then? There was a child! I have a sister?" Montague staggered backwards towards his chair and fell into it.

"She's been found?" he asked.

The two men lowered their gaze. The change in Montague's long-time, no-nonsense employee's body language hit him like a ton of bricks.

"Its not good news, Mr. Stanford."

"Just give it to me straight!" he belted out as his heart pounded his chest.

"Unfortunately, she's been murdered, sir. I am deeply sorry to have to tell you this, Mr. Stanford."

"When? How? And by who?" He grimaced as his heartache quickly turned to anger.

"Recently. It's all over the papers. It was the lady Clay was searching for."

"You mean the murdered Schwab's waitress! Are you sure?"

"Positive, sir."

"After all these years. So close. That's all, gentlemen. Thank you. Do not say a word about this to anyone."

With that the men turned to leave the darkly paneled office. One of the two stopped at the door to look back at his long-time employer.

"So sorry for your loss, Mr. Stanford. Truly." Then he quietly closed the door behind him.

"So, it really was true. All these years … a waitress right here in Hollywood. My God, I probably looked her right in the eyes on one of the few times Cosima and I had lunch there." He propped his elbows up on his desk and buried his face in his hands as if to block out the world for a moment, and cried.

"How could I have failed to find her? My poor dear sister. The life of a goddamn struggling waitress." He was beside himself with grief.

He had dreamed of finding her or him since learning of the half truths as a young man. He had traveled down this terrible road once before.

"Samantha, I don't want to be disturbed until I ring you. No calls, from anyone, not even Cosima or Clay. Take a message."

Trying to pull himself together, he spent the rest of the day tearing through the file given to him by his investigators.

His hurt and grief turned to anger after contemplating her murder. He went from the file to the Internet and voraciously read everything he could about her and her murder.

"All those horrible things the tabloids are saying about you, my sister." He couldn't find it in himself to judge her.

The file also told him that he was an uncle to a 22-year-old niece named Brit Henderson.

Chapter Thirty-Two

NEW LEAF

"Samantha, get Rod on the phone now please. Tell him it's urgent."

Rod was one of his lead attorneys from a team of eight top lawyers in the city that he kept on staff.

"Yes Montague, how are you?"

"Not well. In fact, I am in a very bad mood. I don't have time to discuss it now. I want you to get on the phone to every goddamn tabloid and newspaper in this town, and you make it clear to every little prissy editor running it that if they print one more insult about that murdered Schwab's waitress they will have me to deal with. And I promise them, it won't be pretty. Be prepared to buy them if necessary. That's an order and give it to them verbatim!" This was a rare mood for Montague so his lawyer's only response was action.

Now, he wanted to know what the hell his son knew about this.

"I need to revisit Clay's involvement with this issue." Something in his gut told him his son knew more than what he had been told.

Most importantly, he had to reach out to Dotty's daughter.

"My niece." He moved his lips with barely audible speech.

He thought he should tell Cosima, then thought better of it until he had spoken with Clay.

"Should I speak to the young woman? How do I approach her? She will probably think I'm some kind of rich nut job." Running over in his head how best to make contact with his newly found niece.

* * *

Within a day, not one word was mentioned in any major tabloid or newspaper in the entire city of Los Angeles. Within two days, the story was dead across all national and international wires. It was rare for Montague Stanford to throw his estimated $37-billion-dollar fortune around, but when he did people sat up and listened.

He overcame his hesitancy of contacting Brit out of a paternal drive to protect her from what he knew first hand she was going through.

"Ms. Brit Henderson?" Montague's secretary asked.

"Yes, who's speaking?"

"Hold the line please, one moment." Samantha transferred the call to Montague.

"Hello, Ms. Henderson."

"Yes, who is this. If this is a reporter, I'm hanging up now!"

"No. No, please don't, I'm not a reporter. I am very sorry to spring this on you like this, but I couldn't figure out any other way to do this. I'm your uncle. A lost uncle from your mother's family. I've only recently found out who your mother was."

"Is this some kind of cruel joke?"

Montague lowered his voice in an attempt to sound serious and not choke up.

"Hello?" There was silence.

"Are you still there?" he asked.

Then he heard a small whisper. "Yes."

"I'm Montague Stanford, and—"

"I know," Brit interjected.

"You know? How do you know? I only found out two days ago," he told her.

"I found out two weeks ago, but I wasn't sure you would want anything to do with me," she managed to say.

"Oh my dear child. I am overjoyed! And heartbroken at the same time. You know what I mean. When can we meet. There is so much I have to ask you."

"Whenever you'd like," she told him.

"Do us a favor, don't tell anyone just yet. Otherwise, you will be surrounded by newspaper hounds' day and night. How about tomorrow morning about 10:30?"

"OK, where would you like to meet?" she asked.

"I'll send a car around to pick you up."

"I'd rather meet somewhere public. Just to make sure. OK?

"Of course. How about meeting at my lawyer's office, 9000 Sunset Boulevard? West Hollywood?"

"I know the building. I'll be there at 10:30."

"I'm looking forward to it, Brit. Bye for now!"

Both sat in a daze for a few minutes on opposite ends of the city. Both thinking about how their lives were about to change. Montague, about how much he was going to try to make up the loss of her mother to her. Brit, thought how excited her mother would be.

"She'll never know any of this," she thought. "An incredible life completely lost to my mother forever."

Had all this really happened to her? Perhaps she was in some weird dream and her mother would wake her in time for her UCLA graduation day. One thing was real, her mother was gone … forever.

"I need to find out who killed my mother before I will ever have any peace in life."

* * *

"He told me who he was and wanted to meet me tomorrow morning. Will you come with me? You are about as close to an uncle as I've got," Brit shared with Michael.

"If you need me to be there I will. It might be a good idea to have someone with you. Have you thought about asking your dad?"

"No. I just can't speak to him right now."

"OK, I'll go with you."

They met up and headed over to the meeting on Sunset Boulevard.

"I'm scared to death." She reached for Michael's hand to calm her nervousness.

"Don't be. I'm sure they are nice people. They wanted to meet you after all."

"You're right. I'm also excited just to have some family out side of Dad."

Montague had them brought up through the private entrance.

"This way, Miss Henderson, your uncle is waiting for your upstairs." The assistant extended his hand to her.

"My uncle. I've never had an uncle." Thinking to herself.

Whispering to Michael, "They called him my uncle." Smiling like a little child with excitement.

Brit thought this during her walk through the large offices, which was as surreal as the long walk behind her mother's casket.

A tall well-dressed man stood on one side of the huge double mahogany doors with a statuesque woman in a perfectly tailored gray suit standing at the other door.

"Wow, I feel like I'm meeting the President," she thought

The polished woman and man opened the door to a large office where a man sitting on a large leather couch began to rise.

"Sir, if you would. A few moments alone for them please." Raising an arm to signal for Michael to hold back.

Michael squeezed her arm and motioned for her to go in.

Brit walked into the huge office and the tall man extended his arms to engulf her in a hug. She searched his face for her mother's features, and found her own. She could see a close resemblance of herself in his face.

"Brit, I am overwhelmed to see you," he told her.

"I may have lost my sister, but I have gained a niece … Let me look at you." Montague held her shoulders and stepped back to take her in.

"Wow! I just can't believe it!"

It was more than she could bare. The burden of so much change had reached a peak. She broke down sobbing. Her uncle held her on his shoulder and tried to calm her.

"It's alright. I have walked in your shoes, and I know what you are going through. You will never be alone again. You have your family now."

She finally allowed herself to hug him as if to admit that this was all real.

"You look just like my mother, your grandmother! You'll see. There is an uncanny resemblance," Montague said with a smile of amazement.

"I'm very sorry. I've just been under so much strain lately, and practically alone through all of this, except for my father."

"You have nothing to worry about, ever again. I've ordered those nasty newspapers not to say another mean word about your mother … my dear sister," he added

"Thank you."

"I know all of this is an enormous shock for you. I don't want to overwhelm you with too much too fast. We'll talk business at a later date. You are in for a lot of tremendous changes in your life. I want you to know that I will be there to walk you through every step."

"Thank you, Mr. Stanford."

"Uncle." Montague corrected her.

"Uncle … that sounds nice."

"My dear, I must mention one thing to you, for your own protection. You are now worth a tremendous amount of wealth; therefore, you must be very careful with your safety. Once this gets out to the public, you will have to put your old ways of living behind you. Your safety must be taken into consideration with everything you do. I would feel better if you would let me assign a bodyguard to you when you leave here. You won't even know that he is there, but he will be there if you should need him."

"What do you mean by wealth? For me?" She sounded bewildered.

"Your mother's wealth that she would have inherited automatically goes to you."

"Who's the man accompanying you?" Montague asked.

"He was a friend of my mother's."

Brit introduced Michael and answered a barrage of questions Montague had about his deceased sister.

"I'd like to meet your father, Brit, whenever you are ready."

"I'll let you know. We are all still pretty much in shock over what happened."

"I understand. Is there anything you need or would like for me to take care of right now? Anything at all. I understand your family recently moved. I want you to know that if you would like to find a house of your own, just pick one out and let me know," he offered her.

"Thank you."

"And congratulations on your graduation, that's a huge accomplishment!"

As she and Michael stepped back into the car, it dawned on her what had just happened.

Brit had just gone from being a lonely, lost, heartbroken young girl with very little money and almost no family to one with a family and incredible wealth.

* * *

"Rob, I'll need the documents drawn up reflecting my sister's shares of the estate. The trust will now go to my niece, Brit Stanford Henderson. Everything has been confirmed including the DNA test. Have them ready by the end of the week. Thank you." He felt very good about this.

With that one phone call, his niece became one of the richest women in the world. The phone call also sliced Clay Stanford's expected inheritance in half. Something he was not about to take lightly.

Montague left a message for his son to ring him at once. In the meantime, he'd update his wife on Brit. He needed to find out more about his sister's husband. Apparently, they had lived a very simple life.

Now that he knew she was indeed real, he wondered how this could have happened. What family secrets could have been so bad that a child was given up for adoption? He could not connect the father he knew or his loving mother to something like this. He knew that he may never know. Besides, what good would come of it now? The damage had been done.

"I would have given anything to have had a chance to spend time with her. I wonder if she knew about us? Who were the people that adopted her? How did they get her? Maybe his newly found niece could shed some light on these questions? She must be in utter shock. So much in such a short period of time."

His mind jumped back to his son Clay. He hoped his son was being on the level with him.

* * *

Clay returned his father's call and reached his voicemail.

"Hi, Dad, I got your message. You sounded like it's urgent. I'm heading out to the boat for the weekend. Will be there from Friday on. I'm throwing a little dinner party if you and Mom would like to pop in. Bye, Pop!"

His father sounded a bit strange, irritated almost. Ah, he's probably just busy. He's gonna flip when I tell him that I snagged the Castle Industries deal!" Boasting to himself about his win owed to crooked manipulation and blackmail.

He was gloating over his perceived ruthlessness. It was a pity really, he had a limitless future ahead of him as the handsome, immensely wealthy, and accomplished heir to a great fortune. Why had he succumbed to the toxic addiction of power?

Clay had not yet learned of the fabled tried and true ancient saying, "Absolute power corrupts absolutely." It was too late for him. He had more in common with his conniving waitress aunt than he could have ever dreamed.

"Why should I be forced to share *my* inheritance with someone who was going to take half. A fucking stranger who'd never even met a Stanford! Who cares about what happened in the past. She wasn't entitled to a penny in my book. She had to be removed from the equation. I was simply being pro-active in protecting my assets from a threat." This was how he justified orchestrating the murder of Dotty Henderson. It was a twisted formula he had worked out in his dark brain.

"What exactly did you find out, Clay?" his father asked. "And don't give me that plate of bullshit you tried to serve me earlier. I want to know how and when you found out that Dotty Henderson, the Schwab's waitress, could have been your aunt? Furthermore, I want to know who it was you had on that jet from Mumbai a month ago. I got a call from Interpol and Homeland Security wanting to know why a jet registered to my fleet was flying an undocumented Indian national into the United States without a visa.

"Son, you will be making a colossal mistake if you should ever think you are clever enough to out maneuver me in any capacity at this point in life."

Clay sat listening to his father on the phone with his head down and his hands clasped beneath his chin. One thing he knew for sure, and that was he did not want to ever piss off his father under any circumstances. He carried the force of a nightmare when wronged.

He had to clean this up and clean it up as in yesterday.

"Dad, can I meet you on Monday and explain to you in person what I was trying to do?"

"Fine, I just hope you weren't foolish enough to be involved in anything illegal. God forbid you are connected to what happened to my sister … in any way."

Chapter Thirty-Three

FISHY DELIGHT

"Whew! Man can I use some R&R this weekend on the boat! I think I'll go out early Friday instead of the afternoon. I'll call up that sexy English actress I met at the Emerald gig. The one with the killer body that knocked the socks off of the photographers with that little dip in the pool. Summer, yeah … that's her name. What the hell did I do with her number?"

Clay had his assistant locate Summer's number and put together a small cocktail party for Friday night on the *Cosmos*.

He would occasionally throw an impromptu party with a small bevy of friends from Malibu and the Marina.

"I'd love to come. What time? May I bring a friend?" Summer asked.

"Sure," Clay replied.

"Terrific, thanks!" Summer was laughing at the idea of attending a party on such a huge yacht given by a Stanford. She promptly rang up her handsome lover Gavin and told him to keep Friday night open, that they were going to a party on the Stanford's yacht in Marina Del Rey.

"I guess that little invite is paying off" Gavin smiled to himself after getting her call.

Summer's roles were getting bigger and bigger. Her next role would soundly put her on the Hollywood working actor's list. For that she was proud of herself. And she appreciated the help Gavin had given her. He had been instrumental in strategizing her climb.

"Tell Kazuo that I'll be looking for something special from him this weekend. I've missed his food this week," Clay instructed his assistant.

"Yes sir, Mr. Stanford."

Kazuo met up with Kai on the pier for his weekend supplies as usual.

"Kai, I need something a little special this weekend, maybe a mix of the freshest you have. I've got a party to cook for and Mr. Stanford will be onboard all weekend."

"Got lots of good fresh stuff, some came in just this morning. How about some barracuda? I also have a gift for you that I put together myself … well, with a little help from a new sushi chef. It's to thank you for being such a good customer, Kazuo." Telling just a small white lie.

"Excellent, set up an order for me and throw some fresh eel in there as well."

"This is for you, and this is for Mr. Sanford. It will save you from having to prepare. It just came in this morning."

"Wow … this is a beautiful spread. Are you sure I can't pay you for this?"

"Naw, just let me know what Mr. Stanford thinks of the quality. My friend wants some feedback on his skills."

"You got it, my friend! Load everything up. I gotta get prepped for a party tonight."

With that the food was loaded and chef Kazuo was on his way back to the boat.

Kazuo snacked on the platter that had been made for him and the crew. He was impressed, it was fresh, delicious, and expertly prepared. He couldn't have done a better job himself. He was confident in laying the food out for Mr. Stanford.

* * *

His Saturday began as usual. Clay rose from bed around 9:30 a.m. after enjoying a fun, lighthearted evening. He was a bit disappointed that his targeted English dish had shown up with a lover instead of a girlfriend.

"Make note to self, verify singlehood next time." Reminding himself.

His Saturday routine was to jump on his bike for a quick spin around the Marina and down to the beach and back in time for a healthy, delicious lunch.

"My bike ride will burn up some of this built-up sexual energy. I'll call Sandy to pop in for a little romp today after lunch. She's always good for a good roll in the sack, and she's close by … Santa Monica." Planning his usual day on the water.

Returning from a hard bike ride, Clay was pumped and famished.

"OK, Kazuo, what's on the menu for today? I could eat a whale!" he said while turning on Puccini's *La Traviata*.

"Oh … Mr. Clay, you are in for a special treat today! You will enjoy lunch very much today, sir!" the chef said proudly.

Chef Kazuo laid out the extraordinary platters of seafood that had been prepared and given to him by his seafood supplier. There was eel, lobster, sushi, ceviche, oysters, and two rare treats, barracuda and blowfish (a small serving of which can run $500), both caught, iced, and flown in fresh.

"You've outdone yourself, Kazuo! This is nothing short of wow!" Clay couldn't restrain himself another moment and dug in.

He ate voraciously for almost an hour, making sure he tasted every dish on the table, washing it down with a glass of 2003 Kongsgaard Napa Valley, a favorite Chardonnay from his small vineyard in Napa where the wine is left untouched in the barrel. A process known as "death and resurrection."

* * *

Clay stretched out on the yacht's sun deck to sunbathe and contemplated his recent "accomplishments" and the methods utilized to achieve them. His thoughts switched gears to the pending arrival of his afternoon delight and the carnal pleasure that he intended to partake in.

Fifteen minutes into sunbathing, he retired to his stateroom below.

An hour later Clay lay on the floor of the stateroom writhing in pain. His mouth was on fire and his tongue tingled. He felt numbness, drowsiness, and his speech became incoherent. He was unable to stand and knew he was in serious trouble and needed help fast. Trembling and sweating profusely from his face and forehead, he managed to crawl to the intercom and moan a whispered plea for "help." He remembered there was a banging on the door and then trying to say "hospital" before passing out. The crew was en route to the hospital within minutes of finding him on the floor. He had a pulse, but it was weak and getting weaker with sporadic, desperate attempts at breathing.

"Call his parents, have them meet us at the hospital, extreme emergency!" barked out the ship's captain as they raced to the hospital. Clay was being attended to by the ship's trained onboard nurse who frantically commenced CPR as fluids were pumped into his body via an IV.

"Captain! We're losing him!" yelled the nurse.

The SUV hurled into the emergency room area at a dangerous speed. The hospital had been alerted and had staff on standby upon arrival.

Clay was whisked into the ER where they began attempts to stabilize him.

He died within three minutes of his arrival.

The crew of the *Cosmos* were in a state of absolute shock.

Cosima Stanford had to be sedated after learning of her son's death and becoming hysterical. Montague sobbed like a child as he fell to his knees on the hospital floor. His only child was gone.

Police swarmed the yacht and no one was allowed to board or leave. All 25 crew members were sequestered in the main dining room. The ship's chef, Kazuo, was almost incoherent. He was so upset that his English had broken down. He was sure it was his fault.

"He was just fine at lunch. He ate lunch, sunned for a while, then went down below. He had a young lady guest coming over and I assumed he was getting ready for her visit," he stuttered.

"I was on the deck when my first mate, myself, and a few other crew members heard a faint cry for help come over the intercom. We recognized it as Mr. Stanford's voice immediately, and we rushed to his stateroom and banged on the door. When there was no response, I opened it and found him lying on the floor in a fetal position shaking and sweating profusely. He was almost unconscious. It was evident that he was in serious condition. Our onboard nurse ordered us to proceed to the hospital as fast as possible. Which we did," was the captain's statement.

Montague ordered an autopsy to be done at once, then retreated into seclusion along with Cosima.

The autopsy report concluded that Clay Stanford III had died as a result of a lethal dose of scombroid, tetrodotoxin (a nerve poison 100 times more potent than curare or strychnine), and saxitoxin (the most fearsome and easily the deadliest of the three poisons). One toxic clam or mussel can contain less than 5 milligrams of the lethal, naturally occurring poison that causes paralysis and respiratory failure.

Clay III's body contained 20 milligrams of all three.

All three toxins can be found naturally in certain raw fish. It would be up to the L.A. District Attorney's Office to determine if this was a homicide or accident. The investigation led directly to the ship's chef, Kazuo.

"I tell you, I ate some of the same food," he insisted to the police. He hadn't told them it was from a different platter.

There was no motive for the chef to commit murder. He was well paid, liked his employer, and got along very well with him by all accounts.

Investigating the chain of contact for the digested food led them to the chef's supplier, Kai Miyako.

"Never in 70 years of business has anything like this ever happened!" He was afraid to tell the police that the platters had been gifts from an outside source. That would surely be the end of his family's 70 plus years of business. He kept his mouth shut. He knew that if the seafood was not kept properly refrigerated this could occur. Fault laid squarely upon Kazuo's shoulders, who was not about to mention that he had served his employer food that was prepared by someone else. Kai wasn't going to sacrifice his family's livelihood for Kazuo's mistake.

"Give us a step by step account of the lunch served. Every detail and every person who handled the food from when it arrived to the boat," requested the police.

The police followed up with Kai's employees, who mentioned an individual that had recently become a frequent customer and friend of Kai's.

"Oh him, I forgot about him, officer. In fact, he mentioned that he was studying to become a sushi chef. He basically was an acquaintance and customer." Still not ready to divulge the fact that the he was the one who provided the deadly seafood because the seafood had come from Kai himself.

"I ate some myself, so I am positive it wasn't my seafood that killed that guy," he convinced himself.

"We'll need a description and the name of the school he was attending if you can recall."

"I can tell you right now, he was blond, about 6'1", brown eyes, mustache. That much I am sure of. I am pretty sure he said that he was attending the Tokyo Sushi Academy."

The ex-senator was brunette with blue eyes. The film industry wasn't the only one who knew how to make use of colored contacts and wigs in Hollywood.

A few days later the police revisited the *Cosmos* seafood supplier.

"We've located the Tokyo Sushi Academy ... In Tokyo! There's no branch anywhere in the entire city of Los Angeles."

No trace of the acquaintance could ever be located.

"We boarded the food. I carried the platters myself and stored them. Served them to him for lunch the next day. No one from the party the night before even knew where the galley was, let alone was able to enter it. I served Mr. Stanford his lunch the next day like I always had, right after his bike ride that morning at 11:00 a.m. He did eat some of it on a plate while lying in the sun. He mentioned that he had a young lady coming over and he wanted to catch a few rays before she got here," Kazuo told the police.

"How long was the food sitting in the sun?" asked the detective.

"I really can't say, officer, I was in the galley preparing food. I can tell you it was very hot that day, around 85 degrees at that time of day."

"So the food could have heated up quite rapidly if left lying in the direct sunlight?"

"I suppose it could. Mr. Stanford was eating rather fast at the time so there was no worry about that. I have never had any issue with any of the food I've gotten from my supplier in all the years I've used him," Kazuo stated.

Clay's death was ruled an accident resulting from naturally occurring toxins in seafood while exposed to midday sunlight, a period of the day when the sun's heat is at its peak.

It was a tragedy that Montague and Cosima thought they would not be able to recover from. Their only child and pride and joy was gone.

Clay's death did not, however, halt the investigation into Dotty's murder.

Rocco eventually traced the money used by Max Moriel to Clay III via a subpoenaed document covering his personal bank accounts and indicating he withdrew $9,999 dollars a month prior to Dotty's death. He was apparently aware that any amount under $10,000 did not require reporting to the IRS.

Clay's hired investigator admitted to police and Mr. Stanford that Clay had found out that Dotty was the lost Stanford daughter. This meant that he had lied to his father.

It wasn't long before it became clear that Clay III had carried out Dotty Henderson's heinous murder out of greed to prevent having to share half of the fortune he stood to inherit.

His parents were even more devastated, at first refusing to believe the evidence, but finally realizing that all roads led to Clay III.

"How could this family be rocked with so much tragedy?" was all Montague could muster.

He and Cosima grew closer to Brit in an attempt to replace the loss of Clay.

Montague made sure that Brit received every cent her mother was entitled to under his father's estate codicil. It amounts to billions, enough to place her among the richest people in the world.

Brit had become incredibly generous to the group of Schwab's friends who had been betrayed by her mother's actions. It was they who had come to her rescue when she had little more than a dollar after her mother's death.

Chapter Thirty-Four

NEW WORLD

The tabloids were far more tempered this time around when news leaked out that the murdered Schwab's waitress was the lost daughter of the billionaire Stanford family.

They stuck to the facts surrounding Clay's involvement in the murder.

MOUTH was the first to break the story with it's unusually gentle headline in an attempt to curry favor from the Stanfords, "Lost billions of tragic Schwab's Waitress: The slain Schwab's waitress who was reduced to selling storied to Hollywood tabloids to survive was recently discovered to be the lost sister of the billionaire Stanford family. Family sources have confirmed the relationship via DNA testing. Apparently the child was somehow mixed up and adopted away at birth. The heartbroken family has searched for her since the 1940's. The incredible story predates the tragedy that befell the family's almost total loss of life in the 1956 *Andrea Doria* catastrophe. The only surviving member of the family at the time was thought to be Montague Romeo Stanford. He miraculously escaped unharmed from the demolished cabin where his sister was killed along with his parents, Mr. Clay II and Mrs. Gemma Huntington-Stanford.

"Mrs. Henderson's young daughter, now known as Brit Stanford Henderson, will inherit a massive fortune. Our sources tell us that she has already been reunited with her mother's lost family. The family has been rocked with more than its fair share of tragedy over the years."

National Radar followed with "Down and Out Dotty was due to inherit Billions!"

The papers sales exceeded those of the murder scandal. Brit was unable to continue living in the home her mother had purchased just prior to her death. She was forced to move for a number of reasons. Once her name had been revealed by the press, connecting her to the Stanford's billions, the house was engulfed by reporters and the gawking public. The phone rang constantly with solicitors asking for money or selling products.

Ralph's young girlfriend left him for a younger man, one younger than herself.

He made amends with his daughter and begged her forgiveness. Over time she forgave her father and they helped each other survive the loss of Dotty.

The Stanford estate made clear that Dotty's share went directly to Brit. This prevented the inheritance from being considered community property, therefore excluding Ralph.

Brit generously provided for her father for the rest of his life, which included a home not far from her new Trousdale, Beverly Hills estate. She allowed her father to keep her part of Dotty's estate, and the funds from the sale of Dotty's dream home in Sherman Oaks.

The repaired father-daughter relationship moved forward. Ralph was reluctant to involve himself with the Stanfords out of personal protectiveness of his daughter and a small tinge of jealousy.

* * *

"You think of money differently when you don't have any than when you have so much you can't comprehend it. You begin to realize that it is far less valuable than the sincerity of people who care about you," Brit said, speaking at a private party she hosted at Schwab's for all of her mother's old regulars, including Sam and his new wife Vivien, but excluding Jacques. Who, she had made sure, through her uncle's connections at the U.S. State Department, was promptly deported back to France after paying back taxes amounting to approximately $51,000 dollars.

"When Michael offered me the gift from all of you, it carried with it the weight of a billion dollars. I was at the lowest point in my life. I truly thought that I was not going to make it. How could a person whose mother had just been murdered even get up in the morning and find news stories in tabloids about what a terrible person she was face the world? I know she abused the trust of so many of you, but I am here to tell you she wasn't all bad. Deep down inside she cared for all of you. I can say that because I had to grow up listening about how wonderful all of you were. Day in and day out! All of you are a forgiving bunch, and for that, I am grateful."

They each spoke afterwards expressing their forgiveness of Dotty. The Tripartite went so far as to comment that "the only reason they were still mad at Dotty was that she beat them to the tabloids for all of that money!" That filled the room with laughter.

They noted that she would be sincerely missed as an endearing icon of legendary Schwab's of Hollywood.

When Gavin and Summer had an opportunity to speak they told the group about how they had first notice each other at Schwab's. Dotty had seen them eying each other, but both appeared too shy to make the first move. Dotty stepped in and told Summer that the handsome gentleman over there had paid for her breakfast. When Summer left to thank him, Gavin was confused. They turned to look at Dotty, who just smiled back at them. The ice was broken and we became a "cookin" item, as Dotty used to say.

"We feel like you are all good friends, having seen you here over the years then forging a common bond from this terrible experience. Summer and I would like to announce and invite you to our wedding!" A round of applause filled the restaurant upon the wedding announcement.

Cino and Victoria gave their offering of forgiveness, more for the sake of young Brit's wellbeing than Dotty's. They reserved their announcement of marriage for fear that it would somehow end up in the papers … Schwab's had a history of that happening.

They were married and produced a bambino within 6 months, having had a head start. Cino left "Hollywood Ferrari/Jaguar" for a career making professional cars for the racing circuit. He never once took Victoria up on her pleas to cast him in one of her movies.

"No grazie!" was his repeated reply. Nothing more and nothing less.

They eventually brought a bambina into the world after which Victoria retired from the film business and never looked back. She had made tens of millions over her career. Cino's income had begun to rival hers by becoming one of the most successful race car producers in the world.

Michael Deeves remained one of Brit's most trusted confidants.

"At least I know who truly cared about me before all the millions."

"Huh, it's BILLIONS, my dear one. Billions and don't you ever forget it!" Michael reminded her.

"I know, but it just sounds so weird, Michael. I don't know if I will ever get used to that. Just like everyone else, I used to dream of what it would be like to be a millionaire, never ever thinking it would happen. Well, maybe if I had won the lottery. But, this … not in a billion years!" she told him.

"The reason you must always remember those billions is that having them can make your life wonderful, but they can also make you a target. There are plenty of sharks, shysters, and crooks out there in and out of fancy suits. It's best to develop your third eye going forward."

"My intuition, you mean?"

"Call it what you will, but you'll need it more than ever now. We all need it in life, but not all of us are faced with the same kind of issues billions of dollars brings with it." Hoping she would learn to protect herself.

"Gotcha!"

"My uncle has been fantastic about that. I really trust him, Michael. I mean, he could have fought me over my Mom's share. He saw to it that I received every nickel right from the beginning. One thing for sure, Clay III was not the norm in this family. The family appears to have been intensely close. Perhaps it was because he lost his mother while so young, in that disaster at sea." Speculating on her new family.

Michael's film was an enormous hit commercially, yet panned by the critics. This prompted American International Films, led by Victoria, to offer him a three picture deal. He could have cared less about the film's critics at that point. He was concerned with only one thing when making his first film.

"To be true to my idea and get on the map!" he was proud of saying.

Michael took Brit to his premiere and they made the Hollywood circuit parties. It was a new experience for both of them. So as not to cramp her potential prospects for male companionship, he made clear that his young friend was practically his niece. She demurely smiled, a little disappointed. She liked the idea of Hollywood thinking he was her handsome older companion.

* * *

Brit made a plea for her Aunt Marjorie to come live with her but was rebuffed until her son George had to move out of state for professional purposes. Left alone and facing the prospect of a senior housing, she took Brit up on her offer.

"Auntie, you have given more than you will ever know by telling me the truth about Mom's past. That I can never put a price on. I am forever grateful."

Aunt Marjorie lived to be 102, cared for by around the clock staff in a wing of Brit's home. Her favorite treat was to share a dinner with Brit whenever she was available. Her mind remained sharp and focused until the day she died.

* * *

Ex-Senator Rick Masters used one of his former contacts to secure Brit Stanford Henderson's contact number. Brit had added Stanford to her name as a bow to her mother's true identity.

"Miss Henderson?"

"Speaking, who is this please?"

"I am an old friend of your mother's and I've got a message for you that she wanted you to have. However, I must give it to you in person. It is very sensitive and important."

"What is it?" Curious and annoyed. She had heard all the tricks by now.

"I can't go into detail on the phone; however, suffice to say that I am absolutely sure you will find it to be personally very satisfying after receiving it. May we meet today?"

Something told Brit this was legit. Maybe she had begun to hone her third eye.

"There's a cafe on Sunset Plaza, The Towers. I can meet you there at 12:00 noon. How will I know you?"

"I'll recognize you from your pictures in the papers. Thank you, Miss Henderson. You won't be disappointed."

Rick Masters arrived early, took a seat at a table opposite the one he'd reserved for Brit and waited. Brit was right on time. She sat at the table waiting for the unknown man with whom she had the appointment.

"What more could there be ... please, dear god, let this be some kind of good news," she thought to herself, afraid to think that there could possibly more chaos added to her life.

He allowed 15 minutes to pass to ensure she was alone, then approached her table just as she appeared to prepare to leave.

"Hello, Miss Henderson. I apologize for holding you up." Speaking to her with his eyes barely visible under the brim of his baseball cap in an attempt to conceal his identity.

"Hello, sir, I'm running late for another appointment. This will have to be quick," she told him. A bit perturbed that he was late.

"What I have to give you will, I hope, bring some peace and closure over the murder of your mother and the individual responsible," he stated delicately.

There was a noticeable cringe in her brow when the word murder was spoken. With that, he looked at her compellingly, straight in the eyes, and handed her a small folded slip of paper.

"Good luck to you, Miss." He rose to leave before she had unfolded and read the note. His intention was to allow her to take in the information he'd provide, alone, in solitude. An opportunity to finally sleep peacefully knowing her mother's killer had lost what they had stolen from Dotty, her life.

Brit quickly read the typed writing on the paper.

"Poisoning by tetrodotoxin, a nerve poison 100 times more potent than curare or strychnine. Several varieties of fish can harbor tetrodotoxin in their liver and other organs. Saxitoxin, the most fearsome dinoflagellate byproduct, is similar to tetrodotoxin. Five milligrams of the compound can be lethal. Clay III enjoyed 20 milligrams for his last supper."

The note simply detailed the process that caused the deadly toxin that took the life of Clay. She knew instantly what it meant. Her mother's murderer had himself been assassinated, for unknown reasons, by this mysterious man. A wave of blissful tranquility swept over her tense, beaten down soul.

Brit looked up, searching for the man. He was about to exit the cafe.

"Sir!" she called out.

He stopped but hesitated to turn around, not sure of what her reaction might be, then looked back at her.

"One moment please!" she pleaded as she rushed towards him.

"Yes?" Perplexed and nervous over the extraordinary risk he had just taken.

She reached into her purse and quickly wrote something down, then placed a small piece of folded paper into his hand.

"My mother has a message for you as well." She turned and quickly left.

The ex-senator unfolded the paper to find a personal check made out to the order of blank, for the amount of $1 million dollars. By the time he looked up she had gone.

He had never expected anything of this sort. He had only wanted her to know that the murdering bastard, Clay III, had been dealt the same blow he had arranged for her mother.

Masters smiled to himself and dared to seriously think about that boat in the marina he had been wishfully admiring lately.

Later that year, on a sultry Southern California July evening, Brit was onboard the *Cosmos* with her aunt and uncle enjoying an early evening cocktail party while the yacht slowly motored out to sea on its way to Avalon for the evening. She stood staring out at the marina, the sunset, and all the beautiful sailboats passing by. Thinking about how free she felt when out to sea.

Glancing in the direction of an oncoming yacht she saw a handsome man standing at the helm facing her. As the two yachts passed in close range, the man's face was easily discernible. He gave a long smile and slight wave with one hand to his head as if in a salute. Her eyes continued to follow the familiar looking man until Michael walked up behind her, trying not to startle her.

"You OK?"

"Yeah … just staring at that beautiful boat."

"Which one?"

"That one." Pointing towards the boat with the name on the back "*Killer Fish.*"

With that, Brit turned to face the ocean, let out a sigh of relief then took in a deep breath of wonderful, salty sea air. Thinking to herself, "I hope I see that handsome stranger again."

THE END

ACKNOWLEDGEMENTS

Thanks to the wonderful essence of my sisters and brothers and my extended family. "I'm just lucky I guess."

To my cheerleaders in life, Anna Harmon and Lillis Settles in memoriam.

For the endless support of my close friends: Evan/Ro, Meg, Nancy, Genni, Stefania, Tony, Tim, Rick, Brittny.

And to my superhero godsons, Jake Evan, Connor Sean, Luke Hampton

And my editor and advisor Adam Robinson. All of my incredible design team.

My readers.

The magic of Hollywood.

ABOUT THE AUTHOR

Per Hampton is a passionate storyteller whose roots are in show business and Hollywood. An avid world adventurer, sailor of top secret submarines and sailboats of any kind. Worshiper of science, music and the arts. Believer in the impossible. He's called Rome, London and New York home. Educated in history and communications. Per currently resides in West Hollywood and Costa Smeralda, Italy. At least, until his next adventure.

Look for S & V: Vol. II, in December 2016

31095585R00161

Made in the USA
San Bernardino, CA
02 March 2016